S N WEDDLE

THE Girl IN THE Night

EVERYBODY WANTS A PIECE OF MISS CARO,
BUT SOMEBODY WANTS HER DEAD...

MERED

Mereo Books

1A The Wool Market Dyer Street Cirencester Gloucestershire GL7 2PR
An imprint of Memoirs Publishing www.mereobooks.com

The Girl in the Night

978-1-86151-916-0

First published in Great Britain in 2019
by Mereo Books, an imprint of Memoirs Publishing

The address for Memoirs Publishing Group Limited can be
found at www.memoirspublishing.com

The Memoirs Publishing Group Ltd Reg. No. 7834348

Typeset in 11/16pt Plantin
by Wiltshire Associates Publisher Services Ltd.

Well-behaved women seldom make history

Laurel Thatcher Ulrich

A WARNING

I do declare, this is an honest and truthful account by me, Miss Caroline Shania Mae Kennedy, of my truly terrifying and unexpected experience of one of the most frightening and frightful crimes ever to be perpetrated on mankind. I have written it in my own somewhat distinctive Deep South style, for I am a southern belle above all else, so that it comes over as authentic, and most decidedly my own work. After much angst and self-analysis I have decided to leave nothing out, because I realize that my readers will need to understand all the personal shenanigans I went through if they are ever going to get their heads around the shady world of political intrigue which I found lurking under the surface of polite society.

But don't worry if you can't. This is first and foremost a personal story which happens to include scenes of an intimate nature that have in no way whatsoever been included to further sales, only to illuminate the truth – and if those scenes aren't bad enough, I can only apologize and say 'hush my mouth' for my detailed descriptions of making whoopee with what might be considered to be mostly desirable men, depending on your plate of grits, including occasional full-frontal male nudity. But it ain't all good, there's some science as well. You can't say I didn't warn you.

THE SLEEPING BEAUTY

You really don't know somebody until you've lived with them. I just wish I hadn't accepted his marriage proposal first before moving in together.

So, there I was, a southern belle far away from home. You've heard of an American in Paris – well I was an American in Wolverhampton, presenting traffic reports on Radio Wolfie for Stan The Man's radio show. That guy had so much on air energy he could have powered the entire eastern seaboard on his own. Except no sooner had we moved into our neat little terraced house together in advance of our wedding than Stan suffered a power cut. It was as if somebody had pressed the 'off' button in his head the moment he walked through our front door.

Lordy, how I tried my hardest to restore Stan the Man back to the guy I knew from our lunchtime show, where he had just fizzed with energy. At first I was riddled with guilt, certain his moods were somehow my fault and worrying in the way that women do that there must be something wrong with me for him to be just so goddam *dopey*. Only when people came to visit did he begin to resemble something like his old self, as if he was only happy when he had an audience, and the audience of one I represented didn't really count. But I was going to marry this guy, and a date had been set. Thankfully it was still around eight months away.

Surely it was no more than the usual getting-to-know-you teething troubles? We were still fabulous on air. After all, we were Stan and Caro from the radio, and our relationship had been nurtured by our listeners.

As for our sex life, it was more like a damp squib than a box of fireworks, truth be told. He would barely go through the motions before rolling over to close his eyes and nod off. Not so much a sex addict as a sleep addict. 'Wakey, wakey, rise and shine,' I would whisper breathily into his ear, to no effect. But he didn't shine, and he sure didn't rise.

I don't want to come over as all cocksure, like I think I'm the cat's whiskers, but this wasn't something I'd ever encountered before. Most young gentlemen of my previous acquaintance had only been too happy to remain conscious in my company. And then, if being miserable and lethargic wasn't bad enough, then Stan began trying to control me, especially the clothes I wore, because he was petrified that I might be turning other guys on. How ironic was that? I always dressed as modestly as a Sunday school teacher – well, I had to, to hide the ridiculously curvaceous body nature had chosen to inflict upon me. I had gotten myself caught in a trap, and it was all of Stan's making. It was enough to drive a girl to desperation, because all I'd ever wanted was to live happily ever after with my husband-to-be, regardless of his shortcomings.

It all came to a head when I got a call from Dot, the landlady of our local pub, the Old Bull and Bush, who occasionally offered me shifts behind the bar when staff failed to show there. The money certainly helped us to keep afloat. When she asked me if I could pop over for the late evening shift, I jumped at it with both feet. Stan was out on a public appearance that night, and I figured it would help me to pass the time, chatting to the locals about their troubles, a shoulder for them to cry on while they drank their ale. 'And don't forget to wear something that flatters you,' she said with a giggle. 'Please don't feel you have to, but a touch of cleavage would certainly help you to get more tips.'

I knew I could do with the money – that was for sure – because being a traffic reporter or even a DJ on a local station were no way enough to keep the wolf from the door.

'Why? I'm not sure that would be seemly, Miss Dot,' I reprimanded her in true southern belle style.

'Get over yourself! You've been blessed by nature, so celebrate it and forget all that sexist nonsense. Our lady customers won't mind, it'll be a celebration of femininity, if you will.'

Well, I didn't want to disappoint her, and besides, I figured it might spice things up with Stan when he caught sight of me, and when we got home we could role-play the customer and the busty barmaid. Anything to help get his mojo back.

When I entered the Bush wearing my tight-fitting silk blouse, mostly unbuttoned, a cheer went up in the bar. I cringed with embarrassment, while Dot gave me the thumbs up to help restore my courage. 'If you've got it, flaunt it,' she said. 'It suits you.' Clearly, political correctness hadn't yet reached these parts. Everyone wanted me to be the one pouring their drink, men and women alike. Hadn't these people seen breasts before?

I suppose it came as something of a relief that my new look met with almost everyone's approval, except one miserable guy who walked in looking like a bad day in Tornado Alley – my soon-to-be husband. 'What do you think you're doing?' he said with a forced smile. If looks could kill, I'd have been dead and buried with the wake in full swing.

'But it's traditional, honey,' I said. 'Like Madonna and Guy Ritchie when they lived in the UK, experiencing the English way of life.'

'Why compare yourself with that old slag?'

'She's a legend.'

'A leg end, more like.'

'I thought we could indulge ourselves with a little role play, you pretending to be the dirty customer and me the voluptuous barmaid who wants to do more than pull you a pint.'

'Well, I'd prefer it if you cover up, babes. Just look at the way some of those guys are staring at your chest.'

'And a couple of the ladies too.'

'It's not decent.'

Womanly confidence can be a fragile thing. Shamed by the guy I loved, I ran back home to our nearby house to change into the baggiest and most unappealing old grey sweater I could find.

'Is that sexless enough for you?' I asked Stan upon my return, for the benefit of anybody else within earshot.

'Whoa! Don't blame me, guys!' he replied, addressing the bar. He was obviously desperate not to lose his popularity with the customers. I would love to put it down to good old-fashioned jealousy on his part. I wasn't about to fall out of love with him over something that trivial. And you had to make allowances, because as Tammy Wynette once sang, after all he was just a man.

But that incident in the pub was only the beginning. It was as if my low-cut blouse had released some primeval urge within him to try and de-sexify me – and the more he demanded that I dressed 'decently,' the more I wanted to dress trashier by the day. And that in turn would lead him to interrogate me whenever I'd returned from having some 'me time' about who I might have been seeing, when I'd usually been shopping for some inappropriately sexy outfits which he forbade me to wear. Except when he was out on one of his PAs, when I could give them an airing in the Old Bull and Bush. It was my little act of rebellion, and it helped to keep me sane, and the customers happy.

Of course, Dot approved, if only for the increased takings. 'If only your fiancé would go away more often,' she said. She didn't much appreciate the man who I was about to marry, and never referred to him by name. But he was almost always around me, checking on me, examining my phone, looking at missed calls. I felt imprisoned, but the only crime I'd committed was to be his devoted girlfriend. How dare I look attractive!

I even considered escaping when he was sound asleep in the middle of the night, which was the only time he wasn't monitoring exactly what I was wearing, doing and saying. He was such a heavy sleeper that I sometimes wondered whether he hadn't died.

But then, just when I was at the lowest point of my despair, something quite wonderful happened. This incredible guy moved in next door, and from the first time I saw him, I longed to be in his arms.

Now this wasn't at all like me, because I was committed to treating my upcoming vows seriously, however trapped

I might have felt. It was my duty as a southern belle to honour the man who'd proposed to me. I didn't take any of it lightly. But then I hadn't seen this guy before, had I? He would have tempted a nun. I looked out from our spare bedroom over the garden in awestruck admiration, drinking in this mouth-watering piece of muscle in tight-fitting denims. When he slowly pulled off his sweatshirt to reveal a torso to sigh for, so honed and buffed and masculine... well, it wasn't a question of when or where or why but HOW I was gonna get to know this guy better. Praise the Lord for those trashy new clothes of mine.

In the meantime I devoured him with my eyes through the window, getting a bad attack of the fanny flutters.

'What are you doing up there?' Stan shouted from downstairs.

Drooling over a real man, I wanted to reply, *one who doesn't need to keep his wife or girlfriend under 24-hour surveillance to prove he's male.*

'Just stripping the beds,' I meekly replied instead. That gave me a further fifteen minutes without interruption.

As far as I was concerned, I'd been driven to act this way, because Stan's possessiveness was tipping me right over the edge. I watched the sweat trickle down that broad, manly back as he scythed his way through the overgrown garden, his strong arms sweeping across that jungle of a backyard, so unlike Stan. I wanted to go downstairs that instant and claim this man as my own.

I hunkered down instead so I was hidden by a chair,

my eyes just peeping over the top so I could continue to enjoy the swish of his scythe and the mesmeric movement of his torso. By now he was drenched in sweat. My fingers crept towards the waistband of my jeans and reached down inside. I imagined licking him dry. I began pleasuring myself even more intensely, until I started to moan. I've always been a bit noisy when it comes to sex.

'Are you sure you're OK up there?' I heard Stan enquire.

I wasn't going to let him intrude on my special private moment. 'Couldn't be better,' I shouted down to him. 'I never knew housework could be so much fun.'

'If you say so,' he replied.

Then the phone rang and I heard him take the call. Great, now I could concentrate on my climax. His swagger, his power, his shoulders, his arms, his strength, his butt, his bulge...

'*Oh God!*' I let out a scream like an Eastern European tennis player, and this time the object of my lust heard it. He stopped scything and looked up at me from the garden. I gave him a little wave of the fingers with my free hand, and mouthed 'SPIDER' in an attempt to explain my outburst.

'Just what the hell is going on up there?' shouted Stan, breaking off from his phone call.

'Just a really gross spider,' I called back down to him. 'You know how much I hate the darn things.'

'Do you want me to help you finish it off?'

'No need. I've already seen to it myself,' I replied.

Did you know that the clitoris has 8,000 nerve endings compared with only 4,000 for the penis? Well I'm happy to confirm, it's true.

He continued chatting away to somebody at the radio station while I tried to compose myself and adjusted my clothing as if nothing of any significance had happened.

'Do you want to come into the studios with me, babes?' Stan enquired when I joined him downstairs at the kitchen table. 'They want me to do a one hander.'

'Oh, you'll be good at that. You don't want me interfering, putting you off your stroke,' I said, trying not to laugh.

'But you're welcome to join me, and watch the master at work.'

'I think I'll pass on that. I've got one of my heads coming on.'

'You do look a little flushed,' he said. 'But how are you going to keep yourself occupied without me around?'

'More housework. I'm really getting to like it. It's better than sex.'

And he thought I was joking.

As soon as he was out the door, I sprinted into the kitchen and poured out a giant pitcher of lemonade, accompanied by a plate of chocolate brownies to be delivered on a tray to our neighbour for his delectation and pleasure. How I like that word *pleasure*.

And I didn't hold back. I slipped into one of my silkiest

and most see-through blouses and put on extra mascara and a slash of red lipstick – Stan would have hated it – and swayed from side in the most ridiculously high heels, so inappropriate for a walk in the back garden on a sunny Sunday afternoon, but I was carrying refreshments for this most gorgeous of men.

'Hey neighbour, you look like the kind of guy who could use a drink and a bite to eat,' I said.

He looked up with an expression of surprise on his face, which broke into a lazy, sexy smile as he watched me tottering towards him. 'That's really thoughtful of you,' he said in a deep brown voice. He had a rugged, seasoned look about him that told me he was significantly older than me and Stan. All the better for me – I love older men.

'Oh, just being a good neighbour,' I said. He started to put his shirt back on.

'No need to do that on my account,' I said to him with a shameless grin.

'Well, if it doesn't offend you,' he said, taking it back off again.

'Is that an insect bite?' I couldn't stop myself from saying. I squeezed his bare-naked shoulder to check the damage. 'Do you want me to rub some cream into it?'

'I'm sure it will be OK,' he said, disappointingly.

'And you should be using more sun block on your back. Just hold on a minute.' I sped into the kitchen to collect as many tubes of ointments as I could lay my hands on.

'Some antiseptic for the insect bite,' I said as I applied the cream. 'Unless you want me to suck it out for you?' I could feel nothing but pure muscle under his skin. 'Now I'm gonna massage your back with sun block,' I explained. My hands went on forming imaginary circles on his gloriously sweaty skin for longer than was really necessary. 'You can trust me. I was a volunteer medic in the Atlanta Civil Guard,' I explained.

'Well that's OK then,' he replied.

I also took the opportunity of carrying out my three-point examination – wedding ring, I'm afraid so – big feet and hands, promising – and a tight, pert derriere – well, two out of three ain't bad.

'I think I ought to introduce myself. I'm Larry,' he said, offering me his big hand.

'I'm Caroline, but my friends call me Miss Caro,' I replied.

He squeezed my hand tightly. 'Pleased to meet you Miss Caro,' he said, squeezing me once again.
'You know, I'm sure I've heard your voice before. Not just because you're a yank.'

'I'm from the South actually, raised in Atlanta, Georgia,' I said. 'Gone With The Wind and all that – just think of me as Scarlett O'Hara without the racism.'

'That's it. I've got it. You sound exactly like that gorgeous woman on the radio. You know, the one who's on with that idiot at lunchtime.'

'Yeah, Stan's my fiancé,' I said, chuckling.

'Oh dear,' he said, smiling. 'I didn't mean any offence. Fancy me living next door to a celebrity.'

'And I'm sure he would like to meet you,' I replied.

'No, not him, you're the famous one.'

'Well, I'm sure he'd like to meet you anyway,' I replied. I could feel myself colouring up.

'Why not? I'd be delighted.'

'So – what about this evening then? '

'Great – I'll bring a bottle of wine.'

'That would be lovely. And your wife too?' I said casting a look in the direction of his ring finger.

'She's not around, I'm afraid. We're taking a break from one another. I'm moving in here alone while she and the kids stay at home in Lichfield.'

'Oh, what a shame,' I said, struggling to hide my elation. I would have him all to myself, 'cept for Stan of course.

Stan was not best pleased when I told him I had invited the new neighbour for drinks. 'Oh God, I'm shattered,' he said. He was always tired, except when he was sleeping. 'It's not because you fancy him?' he added with a hint of alarm in his voice.

'Now you're being ridiculous. He's old enough to be my... er... older brother. I only invited him because he's on his own. I felt sorry for him, that's all. And it's the neighbourly thing to do, isn't it?'

'In the US maybe, but not here in England. Us Brits

like to keep ourselves to ourselves.'

'And he just loves your show.'

'Oh well, in that case, it would be rude not to,' he said.

Larry turned up with an expensive bottle of burgundy in one hand and a big bouquet of flowers for me in the other. After Stan had bored him senseless with a lengthy history of his career in radio, I probed him about why he'd moved in next door.

'It's complicated,' he said.

'Ain't it always,' I replied.

'My wife and I are having a trial separation after fifteen years of marriage, to see if we can't work things out. I think she's had enough of me.'

'I find that hard to believe,' I said with probably too much force, although Stan only managed to stifle a yawn.

'She gets infuriated by what she describes as my lack of a career plan. I prefer to write about tranquil countryside pursuits, and I edit British Waterways Magazine. She would prefer me to go back to my old career in showbusiness journalism. You can make loads of money writing pointless stories about stupid celebrities, but it doesn't float my boat. I'm a country boy at heart.'

'Ahhhhh,' I sighed.

'Boy, that's pushing it. You must be at least forty,' Stan rudely observed.

'I'm 38 actually. That must seem very ancient to you young people.'

'Trust me, Larry, you're still in your prime. And if that wife of yours is crazy enough not to want you, then pretty girls will be standing in line to carry on where she left off.'

That told him, just in case he was in any doubt.

After that first glorious meeting our paths crossed a couple of times, but Stan was always around. As I lay in bed one night, Larry only a wall's width away, I started imagining what it would be like to sashay into his bedroom, dressed in my trashiest undies, and be ravished by him. Stan was already fast asleep in our bed. He was to sleeping what Stephen Hawking was to black holes – a world expert – and I knew nothing would wake him for the next seven or eight hours.

It was then that I had a wicked thought. Just suppose I did venture next door in the dark to see Larry. Would Stan ever know? He was out for the count, and I had an itch that needed scratching... There was only one thing for it. I was going next door, regardless of the consequences. It was now or never.

I crept out of bed and made my way into the spare room, where I took off my PJs and slipped into a shamelessly provocative animal print lace garter slip. I didn't want to leave Larry in any doubt about the purpose of my call.

I looked up to see a subdued light shining out of his bedroom window. Guided by it, I tiptoed cautiously across our back yard into his. In my right hand I was carrying a bowl. If I was going to run back home, now was my last chance to do it.

I was about to knock lightly on his door when I stopped. What in heaven's name was I doing there? I was an engaged woman with my fiancé sleeping only a short distance away from me. But sometimes a girl has to follow her heart – or was it nothing more than base desire?

I knocked. The door opened in front of me.

'I thought you might want to borrow some sugar?' I said, holding out the bowl to him.

'How kind,' he replied with a knowing smile.

'I want you to fill me full of your spunk,' I said out loud. I only meant to think it, but out it came. I could have died at the horror of my unseemly remark, but it seemed to do the trick regardless. He took me in his muscular arms and pinned me against the wall as we devoured one another with our lips. Then he carried me into his bedroom, right next to where Stan was sleeping on the other side of the wall, and laid me on his bed. He slipped my nightdress above my head and buried his head in my breasts.

When his mouth teased my nipples I wanted to moan so badly, but I didn't want to wake Stan, so I tried to keep it to a murmur, which became ever more difficult as his fingers roamed confidently inside me, playing me like his piano. So unlike Stan, who never quite knew which notes to select, and was invariably out of tune. But when

Larry's tongue ignited my most personal part, causing pulses of pleasure to reverberate through those eight thousand nerve endings, I screamed. In fact I screamed so loudly it shook the window pane.

'Shush!' he gently urged me.

'Don't worry, he'll be fast asleep,' I reassured him, and he proceeded to explore every inch of my body until I was alive with sex. I couldn't contain myself any longer. I put my hands down his Calvin Kleins like I was unwrapping the best Christmas present ever. It felt exactly the way a real man's should. And it took my breath away as he entered deep and wide inside me, exceeding every girl's expectation of being royally regaled by a mighty sword worthy of Lancelot himself.

'I'm dying of pleasure here,' I moaned. He was inhabiting me so completely that I wanted it to become a lifestyle. And after what seemed like an eternity of relentless lovemaking, yet blissfully gentle when the moment required it, we both came in unison with joyous whoops worthy of a Wild West show, and then lay peacefully in one another's arms while I stroked his big strong arms.

Truly, I had been ravished.

'So where do we go from here?' he asked.

'I could stroke your humongous balls,' I replied, which was all it took to set us off again.

What a man! So we made love again, although rather

more tenderly this time around, and for even longer. I wouldn't have believed that was possible.

We both knew that life could never be the same for us again, although I still made sure to get back to my own bed before Stan awoke. I changed into my PJs and looked as innocent as a harlot can.

'Did you sleep well?' Stan asked.

'Never better,' I replied and left it at that.

After that Larry and I met up every night, and if anything, the sex got sexier. In between we even found time to talk. He spoke so tenderly of his concerns over the effect the trial separation might be having on his two children, while he was happy to listen to me blathering on about my worries regarding Stan, never feeling the need to come up with definitive answers.

We even got to spend time together on Larry's narrowboat when Stan was called away to receive a special radio award in London. It's a wonder we didn't sink the darn thing, what with all our rocking and rolling. I can safely say it was the happiest time of my life. Even Dot in the pub commented on how good we looked together, and she wasn't talking about Stan.

'But I feel so guilty,' I told her at the end of one of my shifts.

'Sometimes a girl has to look elsewhere when there's a man who's lacking at home,' she said.

'I do declare Miss Dot, you are without doubt a decidedly bad influence on me!' I told her.

Then one night Larry proudly announced after we'd made love that he'd finally decided to leave his wife for me. That's when the enormity of what I was doing began to kick in. I was drowning in guilt. I suddenly felt I'd committed a dreadful sin by sleeping with Larry and now I must atone by marrying Stan.

'I'm so sorry, but I'm going to have to end this,' I told Larry one night. 'I've made a commitment to Stan and I can't let him down.'

He begged me to see sense, but nothing anybody could say could make me change my mind – not even Dot. 'You two were made for each other and you've got your whole life ahead of you,' she pleaded with me. 'And he's got humungous balls.'

'Miss Dot!' I exclaimed in shock and surprise. When did I ever tell her that?

Still I refused to give up on my fiancé, although I was truly astonished when Stan announced that Larry had accepted his invitation to become Best Man.

'Oh great! I didn't think you were that keen on him,' I said, trying to disguise how angry I was that Larry had agreed to the request. What the hell was he playing at? Maybe that's what fired me up to ask Dot to give me away, and surprisingly she agreed, without any reservations about whether I was doing the right thing.

When the big day arrived, I hardly noticed Stan as I

walked up the aisle in the wedding suite of the George Hotel, but Larry looked so super-handsome I could barely take my eyes off him. What in the name of God's little green apples was I doing getting married to Stan? This was a whole lot crazier than nipping next door to ravish my neighbour while my fiancé slept alone in our marital bed. Yet I was determined to go through with this wedding, however insane it might seem, to wash myself clean of the guilt of forsaking Stan for Larry's arms.

Yet I still wanted one last act of defiance, which is why I showed up in a rebelliously red taffeta wedding dress, designed to shake Stan to his core. You should have seen his face, and Larry's too, though for different reasons, I guess – Stan, with trepidation for what he was about to take on, and Larry for what he could have confidently enjoyed but was about to forsake.

When the registrar began to read the oath asking my fiancé to pledge his love for me, a strange thing happened – Stan stayed resolutely silent. What was he playing at?

The registrar leaned forward and mouthed 'say I will' at Stan, but still he refused to say it.
Instead he drew a deep breath and solemnly declared, 'it's more a case of I won't.'

'Stan? How could you?' I stared at him, my eyes like daggers on stalks.

'Sorry babes,' he said. 'I know how crazy you are for me, and just how much it will break your heart, but I'm really not sure I can deal with the whole commitment thing. It took a very wise woman called Dot to convince me that I wasn't ready to be a husband to you – or anybody else for that matter.'

So it was Dot who'd talked him out of it. I could have killed her and hugged her at the same time, mostly the latter, once I'd got over the shock.

I took Stan's hand, looking at him more warmly than any time since hed first proposed to me, live on air. 'Maybe you're right Stan, and it just wasn't meant to be, although a heads up about your intentions would have been nice.'

'You're so right babes,' he honestly replied. 'I'll tell you what – I'll play a few tunes for you at our reception as my way of saying sorry. No charge, it's on me.'

'Reception? How on earth can we have a reception when you just jilted me at the altar?

'It's a shame to see it go to waste.'

'If you say so,' I lamely replied.

'Frankly my dear, I don't give a damn about the reception' said Larry, intervening out of the blue. He looked mighty fine in his black Pierre Cardin suit. 'if you're not ready for her Stan, then I most certainly am,' he said. Then he walked purposefully towards me and went down on one knee. 'Caroline Shania Mae Kennedy, will you do the honour of becoming my wife?' he asked.

I decided I'd best keep him waiting. Well, just for a second or two. I put my index finger under my chin and looked up at the ceiling with my head prettily tilted to one side in the customary pose of a well-brought-up southern belle who has just been asked for her hand in marriage.

'It's true, you are the best man, by some distance – sorry Stan,' I said as the guests looked on in astonishment. 'Fiddle-di-dee, I do believe I will accept your proposal most willingly, kind sir,' I eventually replied, milking every last second. The guests, who had been on something of an emotional roller coaster, cheered wildly, mostly in relief.

I mouthed a 'thank you' towards Miss Dot, tears welling up in my eyes. And then we all trooped off to the hotel's Great Hall, where Stan played a selection of hits from the eighties while Larry and I took to the floor for the first dance, no longer having to hide our love away. We danced to one song after another before we finally snuck off to the bridal suite. Not that we were married yet, although it was only a matter of time. Or so I foolishly believed.

PART ONE

INTO THE PLIGHT

CHAPTER ONE

'Unseasonably warm for the time of the year,' I said to the commissionaire in my best mock English accent as I sashayed into the studios of Capital Talk, London's number one speech-based station. How British I'd become, yakking on about weather when a simple 'Hi y'all!' would have got me through the door. Maybe I was still trying too hard to fit in, even after five years in the UK. I had long since learnt that England was a peculiarly foreign land, and despite the fact that they speak something vaguely similar to American, nothing can hide the differences between our two nations.

And before you go hollering to the Station Manager, yes, I am well aware there is no such thing as an American language. I speak mostly Deep South, anyway, while

American English is the most those pesky Brits will concede – and I have to keep on the right side of them, seeing as I have the honor of being a presenter on 'Into the Night,' London's top-rated late-night radio talk show. You see, they don't take too kindly to Americans taking over the airwaves over here, forgetting that we've had to endure the likes of Piers Morgan and Simon Cowell for our sins. But some place along the way they'd had to get used to my southern drawl, since I'd inherited this hallowed slot from a buttoned-up British guy who used to spend most his airtime talking about how chocolate bars had shrunk and strawberries had lost their taste since he was a kid.

'Hi y'all! It's Tuesday night in good ol' London Town and I'm feelin' friskier than a cat whose milk's been spiked with moonshine' I said, exploiting every last darn ounce of southernness I had at my disposal. Don't judge – these Brits couldn't get enough of it. 'Now don't let me catch you nodding off, 'cos sleep is for wimps. I need your attention for our big debate, because tonight we're going the whole hog.'

Apparently, according to our Station Manager, Carla, research had proved that guys found my accent to be 'irresistibly sexy,' while women admired that hint of 'knowing submissiveness' while still remaining in control. So that's what all the fuss was about. And not only was Carla my boss, we'd gotten as close as two fleas on a dog's nose through our shared adventures hanging out together in the West Country media, long before she became a big bad boss. Not that I was obliged to agree with her on every aspect of broadcasting – she thought conspiracy theories could make good radio, whereas I'd been trying to cleanse Into The Night of all those annoying idiots who longed to share their thoughts about working for the Man, the Illuminati as the real rulers of the world (not governments) and President Trump being the advance guard of an alien invasion by lizards. OK, I may have had a little sympathy for that last one.

'I've got Dean on the line,' said Tom, my technical assistant, through talkback during the commercial break. He fancied himself as producer, and much more besides.

'Tom, I told you never to put him on air again. What a fandango in a farmyard that was!'

'You mean when he argued that cats are secretly planning to take over the world, and were about to start suffocating their owners one by one in their sleep? That was utterly brilliant.'

'Only if you're a moron,' I replied.

He had as much chance of becoming a producer as I had of marrying Prince Harry. I certainly had no time for him personally, even though he was straight-backed, wide-shouldered and long in the leg, with a peachy bottom that just cried out to be pinched. That was mostly because I'd always preferred older men, but with 30 fast approaching, maybe I was running out of runway when it came to ensnaring a mature Mr Right. In truth, I'd given up on older men ever since I spilt from Larry, the man who'd broken my heart, some five years ago now. Predictably, he'd gone running back to his wife after he came to my wedding and promised to marry me – yes, it was a little complicated.

No sooner had he returned wifewards than I hightailed it out of Wolverhampton, where I'd been presenting traffic reports on Radio Wolfie, to disappear to the more scenic West Country, where I set about trying to forget by knocking back too much booze and partaking of too many inappropriate men. What's worse, I became a weather girl on local TV to totally deaden the senses. And you should have seen some of the outfits my Neanderthal boss expected me to wear. Perhaps unsurprisingly, I soon got a following mostly among dads and lads, and it wasn't long before I was invited to make public appearances at sports clubs to judge their Player of The Year or Surfer Boy of the Season. Not that it paid well, but I could just about afford it – how else was I going to meet so many fit guys? You see, I had a bad case of I'm Going To Wash That Man Right Out Of My Hair, and I was using other guys as my shampoo. He'd really broken my heart big time, you know, the one who'd proposed marriage to me at my wedding to somebody else entirely, after the groom had lost the plot and backed out. It was quite a fandango, I can tell you, but how thoughtful of Larry to save me from my embarrassment and propose marriage instead. How romantic was that? OK, so he was already married to somebody else, but on a break from his wife, which kind of made it all right, according to my moral compass. Which was overdue a repair, as you might have guessed.

So, after all that kerfuffle he only goes and dumps me, and instead of forsaking all others I embraced them, using each one as a spit in the eye for Larry. It was just a phase, I guess. At least I was now picking and choosing, and no longer dependent on the whims of an indecisive middle-aged man, which was more than could be said for my so-called career. Even in the depths of winter my pervy old-school boss would find increasingly bizarre excuses for me to strip off on air – political correctness hadn't yet taken hold in Barnstaple – whether it was enrolling for a new school for pole dancers while revealing tomorrow's weather upside down in a basque or sashaying down the cat walk in a bra and thong waving isobars in the air. I suppose I could have objected, but as a meteorologist I have to tell y'all I made a great Barbie.

Sadly, my radio job wasn't any higher minded. I was linking hits on Jolly Roger FM in between saying suggestive stuff about rubber ducks at bathtime in my sexiest southern belle delivery. Not exactly what Guglielmo Marconi had in mind when he first started sending radio signals – or maybe it was? You know what Italian men are like. And most of the time, there was my friend Carla in the background, telling me 'you're better than this, Caro,' while behaving just as badly herself.

It was not until I delivered the forecast dressed as an

Egyptian belly dancer being fed grapes by a bunch of burly beach bums that I had my moment of truth and rediscovered shame.

'You can take your grapes and stick them up your jock straps,' I proclaimed with almost religious zeal as I stormed out of the room, wobbling like a tipsy Cleopatra on my stiletto heels and vowing to myself never ever to have anything more to do with Trash TV and Radio. I was free at last. I would never allow myself to be defined by my curves any more. I was going to get myself a position in quality broadcasting. I would wipe out all those meaningless encounters with men from my private life and be wedded to my career instead.

'I'll give it three weeks,' said Carla when I told her. Sometimes you have to ask yourself, what is the point of friends?

Of course, it was all right for her by then, all loved up with a partner who adored her, now that she'd finally accepted it was a woman who could best float her boat. Of course, I'd considered that – who hasn't? – especially after Larry did the dirty on me, as if the entire male sex should pay for his crime. But it wasn't to be, whereas for Carla, as her personal life became more fulfilling, her career soared. She got a management job with Exeter FM before finally making it to Chief Executive at Capital Talk, London's number one speech station. I don't deny that it's helpful to have friends in high places, so it wasn't long before I came knocking on Carla's door.

Now I had the opportunity to try my hand at something worthwhile and meaningful, discussing the issues that really mattered to people and becoming the kind of woman that Larry would admire and look up to – although I was going to reject him this time around, just as I would Tom, my technical operator, who was driving my show (he'd been trying to hit on me for weeks). And just because I found him vaguely attractive didn't mean I had to sleep with him, did it? I daydreamed about him instead – far less messy that way – and imagining what this fine six-foot specimen would look like naked. Well, it had been six months since I'd last played hide the sausage. While I was picturing him, locked away in my own little bubble of consciousness, I suddenly became aware of the real Tom hollering into my headphones like a guy possessed.

'You're on air, Caro – what the hell is wrong with you?' I heard him say. He was lining up the next caller, saying he was called Harry.

'Hello Larry,' I mistakenly said, maybe subconsciously thinking I might be speaking to the love of my life after all these years.

'It's Harry,' Tom said, laughing.

'Not Prince Harry? I had dinner with him once.'

'You can call me Larry, or Prince Harry. I'll be whatever you want me to be,' he replied, his voice going deeper, and the breathing heavier.

A red rash appeared around my neck, and Tom quickly

aborted the call by activating the jingle we played when callers went slightly off-piste, followed by commercials for loans, garden sheds and preventing gas. I guess that was our typical Capital Talk listener, sitting alone in his shed, counting his borrowed money and farting. Nice!

'There's another one for my YouTube hall of shame,' I said, expecting some comforting words of consolation from Tom, who was supposed to be on my side, let's not forget.

'What were you thinking of? No, don't answer that. I'd rather not know about your fantasies. You've already made it perfectly clear I'm not like to get the chance to fulfill one of them.'

'It's not all about you. I'm through with men, period.'

'As if,' he replied.

Why do men still go figuring they are so darn indispensable? Fish and bicycles came to mind.

'Standby, we're back on air in… three, two, one,' said Tom.

'Welcome back to my front porch,' I began. 'Why don't you just pull up a chair, take off them there boots and make yourself comfortable while we talk Into the Night.' Tom gave me the thumbs-up sign, visibly relieved that I was starting to resemble a broadcaster again.

'There's a report comin' out tomorrow' (notice how I'm so up to the minute) 'which worryingly reveals' (caring, too) 'how young men just can't confide in their male friends about their deepest concerns, mostly because of their fear of being laughed at. Ain't that the truth, Tom?'

I would occasionally drag him into the debate when the mood took me, happy to throw him the occasional curve ball, just to see how he would play it – mischievous really.

'Do you know what I think, Miss Caro? Male friends are strictly for drinking beer, having laughs, or trying to outdo one another about who's got the fastest car, or whose girlfriend has got the biggest boobs, or the most luscious lips, or the shapeliest legs.'

'So you're not exactly what they call a new man, Tom,' I observed.

'No way! And if you were on my arm reckon I'd be crowing about you to the boys, Miss Caro.'

'In your dreams,' I replied.

And just in case you think I have a mighty high opinion of myself, it's what we called banter, and a requirement of the job was to big up my image as the curvaceous siren from the South. OK, I hadn't quite made Newsnight yet, but I was getting there.

'Then it's a lonely old business being a guy, at least as far as Tom is concerned. Who would like to open up out there and tell me something they wouldn't tell their best friend? We'll be right back.'

'Now you've done it,' said Tom over the talkback. 'Every sad case this side of Neasden will be calling in to tell us the size of their dick. Not exactly elevating radio, is it?'

'What an unfeasibly low opinion you have of your own sex,' I chided him.

'Back on air in three, two, one,' Tom announced.

'If you can't open up to your best buddy, then why not try me? Call in to Miss Caro. Colin on line three, what would you like to tell me?'

'It's Harry actually...'

'No you don't,' I replied as Tom triggered the caller ejector seat.

'And what have you got for us, Phil on line three?'

'I've got three testicles,' he proudly announced.

'Oh, a pair and a spare,' I said as Tom cut him dead too.

Something told me that this particular edition of my radio show was not heading for a Sony Radio Award, unless it perked up pretty darn soon.

'It's all going very well,' said Tom on the talkback, but I wasn't giving up yet.

'Dennis on line two – and what is it that you would like to reveal to me?'

A pause can seem like a lifetime on live radio, whereas this one went on so long it could have been eternity.

'Hello Dennis,' I said. 'I can hear you breathing, which is a good start – are you still there?'

'He's probably plucking up the courage to tell you he's got a small penis,' said Tom through my headphones.

And then Dennis spoke. 'I've got a secret that's so shocking that if I told you, somebody would have to kill us both, not to mention all of your listeners.'

'So, he hasn't got a small penis then. That's a relief,' said Tom, who had mistakenly hit the on air button, so all of London was listening.

'Well, I have, as it happens,' said Dennis, 'but I can't see what that has to do with anything.'

'Nothing whatsoever,' I said in the hope of consoling him, 'although it can't be easy, Dennis, can it?' I was trying to draw him out. 'I mean, if you'd like to talk about it. I can be caring, whereas most girls struggle not to laugh out loud – am I right?'

I'd discuss almost anything to avoid another conspiracy theory.

They can be so cruel, can't they? You're probably wondering whether size matters. Well, truth is, for most girls it can be a deal breaker, even though some won't admit it. So how does that make you feel?'

This is where I expected him to pour his heart out, to prove that men can express their feelings too. But all I got was silence.

'OK? Maybe that's for another show'.

'There probably won't be another show, if what I'm about to tell you comes to pass,' he said ominously. Either he was from the Independent Radio Authority and had been monitoring us, in which case he could well be right, or he was about to go all conspiracy on me.

'Take 9/11,' he said.

'I'd really rather not,' I begged him. 'Nor do I want

to talk about how Aids was manufactured by giant pharmaceuticals, or the curious death of Princess Diana in the night, or the absolute power of the Bilderberg Group subverting democracies everywhere.'

'Why ever not?' he replied, as if I'd just said the most ridiculous thing imaginable.

'Because I know hogwash when I smell it,' I replied.

'Ah… you've been warned off, just like all the other presenters at your station, only wanting to discuss issues that won't upset the new world order. You'd rather concentrate on trivia, the new opiate of the people.'

'I'll have you know sir, we only talk about issues that matter here on Capital Talk.'

'You're censoring me, then?'

'So, what is it you'd like to say?'

'You'll only go and cut me off.'

'No more penis jokes,' said Tom on talkback. I can't say I wasn't tempted.

'No, I totally won't – the air is yours.'

'OK. On the morning of 9/11, there wasn't a cloud in the sky, whereas now there are clouds everywhere, yet it never rains.'

'Weather changes – I should know – I used to be a weather girl.'

'Yes, I've seen you on YouTube, making an exhibition of yourself.'

'I can only apologize.'

'Great boobs though.'

'Well thank you, kind sir.' What else was I supposed to say?

'Am I still on air?' Dennis asked.

'Sure thing, honey,' I replied.

'This is going absolutely nowhere,' said Tom over talkback as he activated the Into The Night jingle.

'But he's still there for you, if you want him back,' I heard Tom advise me during the commercials – and for one moment I thought he was referring to Larry, the love of my life, so obsessed had I become.

'I'll be darned if listeners think I've been trying to censor him. Bring him back for more,' I instructed Tom.

'But keep it short, like his dick. I can hear the sound of radios being switched off all along the North Circular Road.' I nodded in agreement.

'We're back, and still on the line, it's Dennis from Lewisham.'

'I told him not to mention my location,' he replied grumpily.

'And when you're not dreaming up conspiracies, what is it you do, Dennis?'

'I follow clouds, and last Friday I saw a cloud formation that was so wrong I almost stopped breathing.'

'Go on.'

'It was what's called an Asperitas. It's Latin for roughness – a reference to stormy seas.'

I can't deny that he was a cut above the usual kind of conspiracy nut job who calls Radio Stations at two in the morning.

'So, in one sentence – what does it all mean?'

'Unless it's a naturally occurring phenomenon, it's either a consequence of global warming, or someone, somewhere, is trying to control the weather – and he who controls the weather controls the world.'

'Cripes,' I said, 'but we're running out of time, Dennis.'

'Not necessarily. One day soon, it will be possible to live forever, but don't let's go there, because there are dark forces at work.'

Now I'd really had enough. I gave Tom the cutthroat sign and he responded by cueing in the X Files theme and bringing it up under Dennis's voice. It was one of those nights, but weren't they all.

CHAPTER TWO

And so, we journeyed on, ever further into the night, to our third hour, when all the truly crazy people would come out to play. Take the next caller, Olaf the Polish trucker, one of our regulars, who'd called to admit that he didn't know how to talk to attractive females, and sometimes lost the power of speech when in the presence of great beauty.

'Well you're doing OK with Miss Caro,' Tom teased him.

'But Miss Caro's different, even though she's the most lovely bitch in the whole wide world, and that includes all of East Europe where I go loads, yet always I can talk to her.'

'That's nearly the loveliest thing anybody has ever said to me, Olaf. You sure know how to flatter a girl.'

'I've got sexy pictures of you all over my cab. I'm looking at your bare ass right now,' he said. His breathing had become noticeably heavier too.

'Are you parked up, Olaf?' I asked him.

'Oh yes,' he replied, although I'm not entirely sure it was a response to my question.

Best let him go. Then it was nice to get a female caller for a change, the first of many to lament their men's inability to open up and express their feelings to them.

'If only I knew what he was really thinking. You need to be a mind reader if you live with a man,' said Rita from Tottenham, speaking for women everywhere.

At least we'd finished on a high, although this was the moment I genuinely dreaded when I had to hand over to my control freak of an ex-fiancé, Stan the Man. Stan's show followed mine, and it was kind of awkward, as I gave him the big build-up, introducing him as the man who'd taught me everything I knew about radio. It was probably my way of handling the guilt I still felt for having cheated on Stan with Larry.

'I taught you well,' he replied in his typically pompous way before moving on to his misery of a show. 'Tonight, we meet a man who's been divorced three times by the same woman – when will he ever learn? – and we talk to a Buddhist monk who's given up the pleasures of the flesh for a celibate life in a monastery, after discovering that his seemingly respectable wife has been working as a high-class hooker in Kensington.'

I couldn't help but wonder whether his choice of subjects had anything to do with our break-up. He claimed that he didn't bear any grudges – well, why should he, considering he never knew about Larry and me, thanks to his heavy sleeping? – which was why he offered me a room in his lovely North London home left to him by a rich elderly aunt at a rock bottom rent.

I can't deny that it had crossed my mind to wonder whether him giving me a place to live was all part of some fiendish plan to lure me back into his life again, maybe as his fiancé once more, knowing I could never have afforded a decent home in pricey London without his help. I had my suspicions, because manipulative was his middle name. Was he trying to reel me back in by exploiting my need for some place affordable to live, or had he really gone from control freak fiancé to laid-back landlord who'd truly moved on? Of course, I worried that I might be abusing his hospitality by giving him false hope, but a girl's got to have a roof over her head.

If only he could have found another girlfriend to cuddle up to at night – not that he was a cuddlesome kind of guy.

Yet maybe Stan had already struck lucky. I had seen a bright red lipstick and a stick of mascara by the bathroom mirror on certain nights of the week, not to mention a black strapless bra and silk panties which I spotted draped over the back of the sofa. He blushed as red as the lipstick when I saw them. 'What's her name, Stan? Anybody I might know? She's got great taste in lingerie,' I said. He quickly changed the subject.

But who needs Stan when you've got Tom on your case, with his moody come-to-bed eyes, that cocky self-assurance, and my particular favorite, his strong, muscular arms, ready to sweep me away to a place of ravishing? I could so easily have submitted to him. He was the kind of guy who'd been put on this earth to make girls giddy with desire – but I was a on a sex diet and he was strictly high calorie. End of!

'Do you want a ride back to Hampstead?' he asked. I knew he lived on the opposite side of town. As if I would put myself in a position where he would feel entitled to take advantage of me.

'That would be perfect,' I replied.

Well, I couldn't afford a taxi, and I wasn't going to endure the night bus again with its human cargo of drunks, druggies and dropouts. What's a girl s'posed to do? And at what age does a woman have to stop saying 'what's a girl s'posed to do'?

'It is a bit out of your way,' I reminded him.

'I could always stay over at yours and drive home after the morning rush hour,' he suggested.

'Nice try, Tommy boy,' I replied. But I accepted his offer. Does that make me a bad person?

It was a real delight to be chauffeured though the

strangely subdued streets of London as one day had ended and another was about to begin. We had become caught in a no man's land of time, apart from the occasional couple, romantically entwined, arm in arm, the odd drunk staggering aimlessly around, or workers in orange jackets on the march to get the day moving again, while our car glided gracefully through the night and into the morning.

'While Stan's away the cat will play,' Tom said full of innuendo. He switched on the radio to hear Stan the Man wittering on about the untrustworthiness of women. I switched it right off again. 'Stan and I are strictly yesterday's news,' I firmly replied. 'I'm not beholden to him, or any man – not even to one who gives me a ride home in his flash new car.'

'Where's the harm in one colleague wanting to do a favor for another by getting her home in the early hours?'

'As long as that's all it is,' I replied.

'But I still can't see what you ever saw in Stan,' he said, trying to provoke me.

'You're only envious of his undeniable charisma,' I said, speaking up for the Man for a change.

'He's got a high-pitched voice, like a girl's. If that's charisma, I'm glad I haven't got it,' he said. He swung the car left from Park Lane into Curzon Street, which sent his wheels a-squealing.

'Hey, what's with the testosterone?' I admonished him.

'More than your Stan, eh?'

'Well that wouldn't be hard.' Maybe I shouldn't have phrased it quite like that.

'So that's why it didn't work out with Stan the so-called Man?'

'So what if he wasn't exactly attentive to a woman's needs in the bedroom? There's more to a grown-up relationship than sex,' I tried to explain to him.

'I just knew it!' said Tom, a touch too triumphantly for my liking. 'But don't get blaming yourself now.'

'I didn't at first – that was until I fell for another guy while we were still together, engaged to be married. But you don't need to know any of this.'

'I so do.'

'OK, if you insist. An older guy happened to move in next door where we used to live. He was on a break from his wife. And from the first time I saw him in his garden from our upstairs window, it wasn't a question of when or where or why but exactly how I was going to get to know him better. He was a real suburban Adonis.'

'Shut up! You're turning me on, and I'm a straight man.'

'Well, imagine what it was like for me, a healthy, heterosexual young woman who had been denied real passion for months.'

'That's when you call a guy like me,' he replied. 'I owe most of my sex life to no-hopers like Stan.'

I didn't doubt it. Maybe I shouldn't have been telling

Tom stuff like this – I didn't want to put ideas in his head, or anywhere else for that matter – but then he couldn't do much about it, stuck behind the wheel of a moving car, so he'd have to darn well listen, wouldn't he?

'Plus, I've always been drawn to manly men. My head must have been some place else when I said yes to Stan. He was no way my usual type, and he didn't have the first clue on how to make me happy. He was so damn controlling, checking up on where I'd been, deciding how I should dress and insisting that I should be with him at all times. I gave thanks he was a heavy sleeper, because that was when I saw Larry, in the night when Stan was asleep. I used to go over next door and have meaningful relations with him, with Stan only a few feet away on the other side of the wall.'

'Wow! You must have been desperate – I mean, felt unloved,' he said.

'But please don't think I'm proud of it, and it's certainly not what I'd intended after Stan the Man asked me to marry him, live on air.'

'Yes, I seem to remember reading about it. It must have been good for ratings, though,' Tom rightly observed.

'After Stan and I moved in together I began to believe that he'd done it purely for publicity, always instructing me what to do at home, while making me feel unloved in the bedroom. He would roll over and go to sleep without so much as a goodnight kiss. And a girl has needs.'

'Now ain't that the truth,' said Tom, playing the role of confidante a little too well.

'Sorry, I can't think why I'm telling you all this.'

'Maybe it's because you want to be reassured that you're not a bad person.'

Empathy, from Tom? Who would have believed it? Add empathy to a sense of humor and those nice strong arms and I'm moving dangerously close to reneging on my sex diet.

'Maybe you're right, Tom. Anyhow, in spite of enjoying the best sex I'd ever had, still I had the moral strength to dump Larry and go through with my wedding to Stan. But then Stan refused to utter the vows at the ceremony, claiming he wasn't ready to go through with it. He left me looking like a complete loser, until Larry popped the question instead. Of course, I said yes to him.'

'Why wouldn't you?' said Tom. We were now getting close to my lodgings, and I expect he imagined that his reward for having to endure me gabbing on would be a night of uncomplicated shagging, without commitment.

'But do you know what, Tom? I never realized you could be such a good listener.'

'I so need to know everything, Caro,' he unbelievably said.

'With Larry, it wasn't just about the sex. I had found a man who had all those old-fashioned masculine values about showing respect towards women, being emotionally strong while being able to fix stuff around the house, rejecting vanity yet keeping his body in great shape, being a selfless lover, bothering to find out exactly how women work, being modest, and making me feel protected, while giving me the space to be me.'

'So how come Larry buggered off too?' he asked.

'If only I knew. It was the same old story. He went back to his wife – don't they always? And before you go accusing me, they were on a break, so it wasn't technically adultery.'

'I guess so,' he replied.

'And just s'posing you're wondering,' I said as he turned into my road, 'I've already been through the sleeping around with inappropriate guys to get over it stage, so that particular boat has sailed.'

'Shame,' he replied, 'although I'm not sure I could have lived up to Larry's great prowess, so maybe it's just as well, even though I'd have been willing to give it my best shot.'

'Good man. I'm proud of you,' I said tapping his arm, 'but you'd have been totally wasting your time'.

'Not even a blow job, which is a minimum requirement, for not only a lift home but having to listen to you going on about your ex, at least in my book of rules.'

'But not mine, which was written in the 21st century,' I retorted as he parked the car outside Stan's lavish house. 'And don't go repeating any of that stuff about Stan.'

'His secret is safe with me,' he said, putting his hand on his heart.

'But it's still a no from me,' I said.

'So, as it seems like I'm just a taxi service, not

forgetting mobile relationship counsellor. Are you going to give me a big tip?'

'I thought you'd already got one of those,' I couldn't resist replying. He launched himself out of his seat, grabbed hold of me with his strong muscular arms and kissed me hard on the lips. I think if the milkman hadn't clinked past just then in his electric cart, I would have been in real danger of surrendering to him, even without flowers.

'Good morning, nice day for it,' he said as I disentangled myself from Tom's embrace and ran inside like the vestal virgin I so obviously wanted to become. I got into my bed alone and soon fell into a deep and satisfying sleep.

It wasn't until the next morning when I turned on Capital Talk News that I discovered that a man had been found shot dead in his apartment in the early hours of the morning, although nobody knew why. It was Dennis, the one who had warned me about strange clouds.

You can't even imagine how I felt, except to say that I ran straight to the bathroom, and hurled.

CHAPTER THREE

As you can appreciate, it was around this time when the fried green tomatoes really hit the fan. I struggled to come to terms with what had happened to poor Dennis. And he wasn't even one of our regulars, just another lone voice who'd called out of the blue to say something strange. Of course, it was obviously a complete coincidence that he'd appeared on my show only minutes before he'd been murdered, regardless of the nonsense he'd been spouting about clouds and other weird phenomenon.

There was so much stuff to deal with in the aftermath of this highly unfortunate incident, even though it had no significant connection with my show, in any meaningful sense whatsoever.

First, I spoke to Carla, who encouraged me to think

about taking time off. 'Big mistake,' I told her. I was afraid it would make people believe there must be a link between Dennis calling in and his unfortunate demise. Maybe that's what she wanted – I wouldn't put it past her.

We even had reporters knocking on the door at home, emboldening Stan to take control – well, that's what he liked doing most of the time we were together – by informing them that I had no comment to make unless they paid a fee. Totally shocking! Since when had he become my agent? Did he want to make it look as if I was trying to make money out of a tragedy? Not my style at all. Having set himself up as my Protector In Chief, he even sent a police inspector away, claiming that I was too stressed to speak to him, and not to return until we'd agreed it. He justified it by saying he didn't think this guy was my type – he was always trying to prove that he was over me by setting me up with inappropriate men.

Another inspector called soon after, only this one was much hotter, or so Stan believed. 'You should see him, Caro, just like that Luther, played by Idris Elba on TV. You're so going to love him,' he said in a rather silly high-pitched voice I'd never heard him use before.

'Stan, it's my civic duty to speak to the cops and it has nothing to do with how hot or not the officers are, although I can't believe they're even bothering to talk to me when I've got virtually nothing worthwhile to tell them.'

That was before I'd been introduced to Detective

Inspector Flowers, who I felt could interrogate me as much as he needed, such was the supremely magnificent athletic body which lay beneath his stylish Paul Smith suit as he stood tall and erect before me. 'Most arresting,' I admitted to Stan. Maybe he did have the taste to fix me up with a hot guy after all.

'It's most kind of you to agree to see me, Miss Kennedy,' said the Inspector. What a nice polite inspector he was.

'It's a pleasure,' I said.

'Oh no, the pleasure's all mine,' he replied.

Don't you believe it, I wanted to say, trying to hide a powerful attack of the fanny flutters. Seeing him standing alongside Stan you wouldn't even have regarded him as being of the same gender as my ex-fiancé in his pinny, about to make us a cup of tea.

'Is he your... er... partner?' Inspector Flowers enquired.

'Oh goodness me, no,' I hastily replied. 'He's my flatmate – nothing more than that, whatsoever,' I heard myself saying.

'That figures,' said the good Inspector, who began to write stuff down in the notepad.

'In fact, I'm not romantically attached at present, Inspector – I s'pose you need to know these things'.

'I'm grateful for your honesty,' said the Inspector in a deep brown voice which beautifully matched the color of his skin. 'Anyway, you can ask me anything you like.'

I couldn't help but notice him taking furtive glances at

me, although it was probably no more than a policeman checking out the validity of my responses, and nothing to do with him having any designs on me. That would be unprofessional, wouldn't it? And unlikely too, as I was sure he must have been tempted by many others far more alluring than I.

'Would you like to see my credentials?' he said. It was as if he could read my mind.

'No that won't be necessary, Inspector. I'm sure your credentials are quite exceptional,' I replied. 'So how can I help you?'

'By answering a few questions'.

Disappointing.

'We need to establish if there was any kind of connection between the gentleman's call to your show and him losing his life,' he said.

'Why should there be a connection? Just one crazy guy ringing in, not long before some even crazier guy breaks into his property to steal his belongings.'

'That's one explanation Miss Kennedy, but we have to explore every avenue before we can dismiss your involvement from our enquiries.'

Holy moley! That was the first time I realised I might just be out of my depth. I directed him to a nearby wicker chair.

'First, I need to ask you one or two questions about the deceased,' he said.

'You mean Dennis from Lewisham,' I said, translating him into radio speak.

'That's the one. Had he ever called in before?'

'I don't think so. I certainly didn't recognize his voice, but then we do receive thousands of calls every week.'

'Have you ever met Dennis face to face?' the Inspector enquired, while I gazed at his large hands, going off-piste again.

'Sorry, what was your question?'

'Did you ever meet Dennis?'

'Most certainly not – it's company policy not to meet our callers.'

'And what did he talk about on air?' Inspector Flowers asked. He was wearing quite large shoes as well.

'Now let me see,' I said, trying to concentrate on the matter in question, 'he was kind of rambling, going all over the place with this and that. I was asking all the guys out there to open up and reveal their secrets to me, and his response was something like, 'I've got a secret so shocking, that if I told you, somebody would have to kill us both, not to mention all of your listeners.'

'You remember it well, then?'

'I find it hard to forget, especially as Capital Talk have been playing that clip all morning, ever since the news broke.'

'And what was your reaction to it at the time?'

'I did think, well that's pretty darn weird, but you do get used to this kind of stuff, the later it gets. And there was a full moon.' The inspector smiled. 'You see, I've been trying to raise the standards on the show. Guys like Dennis just do the opposite with their predictable conspiracy theories.'

'But according to the press, you then went on to talk about the size of his penis?'

'That was all a result of a silly mistake made by my technical operator, Tom. Although when Dennis admitted it, yes, I had hoped he might open up. Anything to stop getting bogged down in another conspiracy discussion, even that.'

'Was there anything else which made him appear different?'

'He did appear to know what he was talking about when it came to cloud formations,' I replied.

'And did he refer to anything of a medical nature, perhaps to do with people living longer?'

'Not that I can recall, although he may have made some reference in passing when I explained that we were running out of time on the show, but it was just a figure of speech, as far as I can remember.'

He told me not to worry, explaining that they would be checking out Capital's digital recording to search for further clues. I could tell I was in good hands – if only! – although I was slightly taken aback when he announced there would be no need for me to have an armed guard, for the moment.

'Holy moley.' I replied.

'I suppse you do have your, er, flatmate.'

'He'd be about as much use as a eunuch in a whore house if the hog shit ever hit the air con.'

'Well, when you put it like that,' said Inspector Flowers, rising to his feet. I suspected he might have been armed – somewhat unusual for the British cops – with something quite impressive. Don't forget, I know how to handle weapons, having served in the Atlanta Military Volunteers back home. It seemed the best place to meet young gentlemen at the time, while doing my civic duty as well. A double whammy, I guess.

He handed me his card on the way out (how gracefully yet confidently he moved), explaining that I could contact him night or day should I have any further concerns, and that he was the only detective I should approach, given his special knowledge of what he described as 'this most unusual case'.

'You'll always be first on my call list,' I reassured him. The kind of thing you say to people who you never expect to see again.

As he leaned forward to shake my hand, for one glorious moment I mistakenly thought he was going to kiss me, and I puckered up my fulsome lips, as they were once described by my art teacher back in my high school days. If that didn't frighten him off, then my embarrassed giggling certainly must have.

Stan seemed more excited about Inspector Flowers' visit than I did. He went on about how I must have enjoyed being 'interrogated' by him, and seemed only too keen to be encouraging me into the arms of another man.

'So, what about your love life, Stanley?' I couldn't resist asking him. 'When am I going to meet the lucky lady?'

'Just as soon as she's ready,' he replied enigmatically. Sometimes I didn't think I knew him at all.

I couldn't wait to tell Carla all about Inspector Flowers, but that would have to wait, as she was my boss above all, and a caller had died on my watch, meaning there would be consequences for both me and the station – which was why I'd been summoned to attend a meeting at Capital House. I got there as quickly as I could, riding the Northern Line as far as Leicester Square, where I picked up a copy of the Evening Standard.

LEWISHAM MAN SHOT DEAD AFTER RADIO HOST IGNORES PLEA FOR HELP

That was the front-page headline. Yikes! Is that what I did? Not quite how I remembered it.

And if that wasn't lurid enough, underneath it read, 'PICTURES INSIDE - the sexy late-night radio siren who mocked a desperate man's claim by joking about the size of his penis'. It really wasn't like that. This didn't sound at all good.

And there was worse. I ripped open the paper to see a gallery of loose women staring back at me. There was a belly dancer, a bikini babe, a girl surrounded by a troupe of naked rugby players in a hot tub.

They were me – all of them. The paper had dug up shots of some of my most infamous poses from my West Country days.

'Darn that asshole!' I said out loud, ignoring the bemused passers-by. Larry, the love of my life, had so grievously let me down, and without that I would never have gone so crazy. And darn that Dennis, who'd only gone and got himself shot after creating a link between me and him, simply by phoning me with some insane story about clouds and governments controlling the weather for their own advantage.

Plus, darn Tom too – I'd told him to steer clear of conspiracy callers, and look what happened when he ignored my warnings. Whose show was it anyway?

But then I thought, darn you Miss Caro, for being more concerned about the press dredging up details of your former life as a provincial sex symbol than the horror of a man losing his life.

'You're probably still in shock,' said Carla. She looked the essence of lesbian chic in her sassy brown blazer, skinny jeans, crew neck sweater and matching canvas shoes. 'Let me pour you a large voddie and tonic.'

'Not too large, I've got a show to do.'

'You won't be going on air tonight, sweetheart.'

'But the show must go on!'

'Over my dead body,' Carla replied.

'Hardly appropriate, given the circumstances, don't you think?'

'There's no way you're going on air,' she replied. Well I was darned if I was going to stay grounded and add fuel to the fire of the conspiracy theorists, who would become even more convinced that I'd had something to do with it.

'You're not in a fit state to go on air,' Carla said. 'I can tell simply by looking at you. I should know, I've known you long enough.'

'Well fiddle-dee-fucking dee!' I raged back at her, stamping my foot in frustration. 'Are you fixin' to fire me?'

'As if! Have you seen the wall-to-wall coverage in tonight's Standard? You're trending everywhere, why would I want to dump you?'

'I had hoped that my performance on the show would be the deciding factor, not this lurid nonsense!' I said, throwing the newspaper to the floor in disgust.

'That's a given,' said Carla.

'How can I ever hope to be taken seriously when all people see is big blonde hair with huge tits and even bigger booty flaunting her sexuality?'

'You think that's bad. Wait until you see tomorrow morning's tabloids.'

'I thought you were supposed to be backing me in raising the tone of my show?'

'That was always the intention Caro, but this is a

game changer. You've gone from a fairly obscure night time radio host to the girl whose name is on everybody's lips.'

A guy gets killed and she sees it as a career opportunity. Was she losing her moral compass, if she ever had one in the first place?

'I hate it when you talk about me like that,' I said. 'I thought you were supposed to be a lesbian feminist…'

'…who's got a station to run, and a friend she wants to propel to the very top of the broadcast firmament.'

Now I could feel my moral compass shifting a little. I was being swayed by the magnetism of fame.

'You've got to look at it like this, Caro. Less is more and all that. Leave them wondering what role you, the sexy siren, played in the death of Dennis, until your innocence has been established beyond all doubt, and then you return in a blaze of glory, possibly to a daytime slot, where you will have a real producer who can help you get to the next level. We might even be talking BBC Radio 2 before too long.'

'And a place on Dancing With The Stars?' I suggested.

'We call it 'Strictly Come Dancing' over here, but who knows?' She had me at BBC Radio 2. 'But above all, as your friend, Caro, you need to take a rest.'

OK, she'd won. I would keep a low profile for a couple of days, while Stan the Man would take over my slot. And I could do with a break, if I was honest with myself. I looked at Carla, queen of all she surveyed, in her swish radio executive's office, and then I thought back to when we first met, the Thelma and Louise of Newquay, two crazy ladies drawn to one another with one overarching aim – to party until we forgot what it was that was making us so darn unhappy in the first place. In my case, it was being betrayed by my ideal man, whereas for Carla, it was sleeping with as many inappropriate men as possible to prove that it was women she really desired. And for Carla it had all worked out, as she had fallen in love with a beautiful girl and they were now blissfully living together, whereas for me, my career meant everything, and that's why I would fight for it, harder than I ever would for any man.

'And you're cool about being home alone at night while Stan's on air?' Carla asked.

'Why shouldn't I be? How could a botched robbery in Lewisham possibly have anything to do with my safety in Hampstead, North London?'

'Who said anything about a robbery? Didn't your dishy detective tell you? Nothing of any value was stolen, apart from a page ripped from his cloud atlas, and the same from a book called "Long Lives".'

'No doubt the thief was disturbed before he could steal anything of any value. And even if he wasn't after money, I still can't see why the intruder would have any interest in me. I am to cloud formations what Graham Norton is to gridiron.'

'You used to be a weather girl.'

'You mean I used to read scripts wearing revealing clothes.'

'Maybe the killer hasn't heard of autocue, and believes you actually know what you're talking about.'

'I thought you were supposed to be reassuring me.'

'I care only for your safety,' she insisted.

'Is that so?' I said, getting up from my chair to pace around the room. 'Having murdered Dennis, why would the assassin want to kill me next? I sp'ose now you'll be claiming it's all part of some great conspiracy.'

'I wouldn't rule it out. I mean, it hasn't rained since heaven knows when – and this is England, for God's sake.'

I sat back in my chair and kicked off my heels. I could see Carla needed some educatin'. 'Conspiracy theories are people's way of reacting to uncertainty and powerlessness in a changing world,' I told her.

'You mean a little like Brexit, or voting for Donald Trump.'

'You've got it, except it's more than that. Apparently, given a handful of dots, our pattern-seeking brains can't seem to resist trying to connect them, to give us some sense of order.'

'You're beginning to sound like you swallowed a dictionary.'

'Just because a girl's curvaceous doesn't mean she can't be clever,' I said. And Carla a feminist too. 'Sure, poor Dennis was the victim of a terrible crime, but a crime nevertheless, which has absolutely nothing to do with me, or any global conspiracy.'

I knew I would sleep easy in my bed, whatever Carla might think. Even Stan said he would take special measures to ensure my safety, which was kind of him, or was it simply a way of attempting to re-establish control of me by keeping me under lock and key? Anyhow, if my lovemaking with Larry couldn't wake him, what chance of him hearing an intruder in the night?

But that was then, while this was now, and just as Carla had promised, I was back on air within forty-eight hours, almost as if nothing untoward had happened. Admittedly, the first night back felt more strained than spaghetti in a colander in anticipation of all those ghouls who'd be tuning in to pounce on those inadvertent clues that might prove I was implicated in the whole sorry mess. While I'd been advised by our legal eagles to avoid any on-air explanations, I was allowed to send my condolences to Dennis's friends and family, and to wish the police every success in their hunt for his killer.

Of course, the newspapers had twisted my words, attacking my lack of concern, their revenge for Stan having denied them access to me, while claiming I'd been offered a hundred-thousand-pound contract to present the weather on Capital TV as a kind of reward for my notoriety. 'HOT RADIO HOST CASHES IN,' one particular headline yelled. Well, it was news to me, because there was no way I was going back to treating my body as my calling card now that I had a thriving journalistic career. Lord only knows what Larry must have thought when he saw me splashed all over the tabloids in my semi-naked state – almost certainly that he'd had a lucky escape, and I couldn't really blame him.

At least I received plenty of support from my first few callers – they always had this exceedingly lovely knack of lifting me up when the going got tough. Take Emma, who launched into a tirade about the unfair way women are treated in the media, following the publication of those compromising pictures of me.

'I guess you could argue that it was only my past catching up with me,' I replied. 'If I hadn't posed for them in the first place then they wouldn't have anything to publish.'

'But those pictures had nothing to do with that dreadful murder, yet still they used them,' Emma came right back at me. 'They would never have published pictures of Stan the Man in his boxer shorts if Dennis had phoned his show instead.'

'You've really cheered me up, Emma,' I said, laughing. 'Incidentally, he wears old-fashioned Y-fronts, not boxers – he'd get lost in a pair of those.'

'Too much information!' she cried out. 'I forgot you guys used to be an item.'

'Oh Lordy, he'll never forgive me. Still size isn't everything, is it?'

'Yeah, and neither is breathing.'

Young women these days – have they no shame?

'Miss Emma!' I said coming over all mock shocked, while she giggled at my exasperation.

I wasn't sure this was what you would call raising programme standards, hoping to move on to something more significant, just so I had something to boast about at my meeting at the Groucho Club with Carla the next day. Maybe she wanted to fire me?

'Have we got something to celebrate?' I couldn't help but ask her after she'd ordered a bottle of Dom Perignon.

'I reckon, although I'm not sure you'll agree,' she replied. That got me wondering. 'I know I'm not your agent, but Capital TV have offered you a contract to present the weather…'

'Oh, to hell with them! Don't they know I've moved on from that kind of stuff?'

'…for a million pounds, which I turned down, on your behalf.'

'I'm so glad, I think. Who wants to be a millionaire, anyway?'

'Phew, that's a relief. I was afraid you might hate me for it.'

'Not a chance, it would have been a backward step. I'm a journalist now, digging out the truth while exploring and challenging the views of my callers, and a personal counsellor too…'

'So relieved you're OK about rejecting that offer then,' she said, 'except they came back with another one.'

'Why can't they just leave me alone?'

'Because you're infamous, and guys love you, while women want to be you,' Carla explained.

'I'm sure you must be confusing me with somebody else.'

'And they doubled the figure.'

'You didn't, did you?...'

'...reject it? Yes.'

'I don't know how I'm supposed to feel.'

'Grateful? Because they doubled it again. And it was at this point I was reminded how I wasn't actually your agent, but your boss – so here it is for you to sign – four million pounds for three appearances a week on our City TV Station.'

I do declare, I was more conflicted than a cooter on crack cocaine.

'So, what would I have to wear?'

'Shall we just say, stuff which flatters your figure. The sponsors are Victoria's Secret.'

'I might have guessed. At least they're tasteful.'

'But it will all be done in a post-modern kind of ironic way.'

I just couldn't see Jeremy Paxman or Larry King selling their souls for mere money, but when Carla reminded me that I would be able to buy my own property in London and no longer be dependent on my ex-fiancé Stan the Man, I reluctantly accepted that sometimes a girl's got to do what a girl's got to do.

'Hand me that contract. And I've still got my radio show?'

'For as long as you want it,' she replied as I signed my credibility away.

Back home, Stan was cool with it at first. 'If you've got it, flaunt it, Caro,' he said. He was encouraging me all the way, so unlike the old days. He used to get so darn jealous if I wore so much as a clingy low-cut top when I was helping out behind the bar, and became obsessed with guys ogling me. But now somebody was crazy enough to pay me four million pounds for it, and once Stan grasped the implications of my financial independence his enthusiasm noticeably waned.

'It's OK honey, I won't have to move out straight away, and we'll see each other at the studios,' I tried to reassure him. 'Anyhow, I'm not so sure it's healthy us still living together, it's probably why neither of us has been able to move on.'

'Now you mention it,' he unenthusiastically agreed.

'And don't think I haven't been grateful for you putting me up, and putting up with me too.'

'I've loved having you here, Caro, I really have.'

Just as I suspected.

"You see, it's my big chance to become a truly independent woman,' I explained.

'How wonderful,' he said wistfully. 'And having been made that fantastic financial offer, I don't think I could have turned it down,' he said, forgetting to add the 'if I was you'.

'I'm not sure they'd hire you to wear a Victoria's Secret basque, Stan,' I said, an outrageous image of him forming in my mind.

'More's the pity,' he replied.

At least he hadn't lost his sense of humor.

'And you know that girlfriend of mine you're always going on about?' said Stan. There was a new tension in his voice and his hand was suddenly shaking a little.

'I can't wait to meet her,' I said.

'Well here's your chance. Caro – it's me.'

I guess some stuff just takes that little bit longer to sink in.

'Oh Lordy – it's you? You're the girl?'

'I so am.'

I gazed at him in shock for moment before recovering myself. 'Well that's just great, if that's what you want to be, 'cos you sure as hell don't make a very convincing guy.'

'That's the nicest thing you've said to me since you moved back in,' he said with a relieved grin.

'Haven't I treated you right? Have I been horrible?'

'Just a bit, but nowhere as horrible as I was to you when we were engaged. I was a monster, but only because I couldn't cut it as your man, and it sent me crazy, seeing every other guy as a threat to us, even though I knew, deep down, we were doomed from the start.'

'So how long have you felt that you were born the wrong sex?'

'For as long as I can remember, but then I tried to fight it, which is why I asked you to marry me.'

'I don't get it.'

'You were just so warm and sexy, and I thought, well if this gorgeous girl can't sort me out, then nobody can.'

'I should be flattered.'

'But when I began to realize nothing could stop me from being who I really was, I became jealous of you. I hated you for your easy femininity, while I struggled so hard to be a man and saw no hope of becoming a girl. And then Larry came on the scene.'

'For which I apologize.'

'Why should you? It was almost a relief.'

'It certainly was for me,' I said, patting him on the arm, and he smiled for the first time in a long while.

'No, not at all.'

'Of course, I was wrong, and had it been nothing more complicated than rampant sex with our horny next-door neighbor making up for what was, er, lacking at home, then maybe you could have forgiven me, but then I go and ruin it all by falling in love with him.'

'Schoolgirl error, Miss Caro,' he said.

'But you should have told me about wanting to be a woman. Hardly a great basis for a marriage, was it?'

'Although we could have had fun painting one another's nails with towels wrapped around our heads,' he joked back at me.

Suddenly I began to like Stan all over again, not as

the man I had known but as the woman I now realized he was destined to become. And I would help her on her way, aiding and assisting her as she attempted to fulfil her dream.

'Let's go shopping,' I said. I figured that with the right hair, clothes and make-up he could convince as a girl, and could even be quite pretty too.

'So you're ok with it?' he asked me.

'Why wouldn't I be? It's who you are. So let's do something predictably girlie to see if you pass the test – some retail therapy, then we'll go for an Italian meal afterwards and flirt with the handsome waiters. I'm strictly for guys, me.'

'Me too,' he replied.

And to think, he nearly became my husband.

CHAPTER FOUR

Not long after Stan and I had our big conversation, he decided to take two weeks' leave and attend a residential course on how to think, move, and behave like a lady. Two weeks, for a man? Twenty-eight years of being female and I still wasn't sure whether I'd really cracked it. Regardless, I gave him my blessing, glad for him to be heading towards his dream in a time when mercifully being transgender was no longer considered wrong.

Also, I was happy to have some time on my own after everything I'd been through, and to re-read Gone With The Wind, the southern belle's bible on how to live life, apart from the outdated racism of course. And just when I got to the part where the Yankee soldier is lurking downstairs at Tara with evil intent, I dropped off to sleep in my exceedingly comfortable bed, the much-needed treat of a night-time presenter on her evening off.

I'd been luxuriating in unconsciousness for a while when I awoke with a start, having heard something go seriously bump in the night. Maybe Stan had returned unexpectedly from his cross-dressing course, or perhaps I was replaying the movements of the Yankee soldier from my book and dreaming the whole darn thing. But then, just as sleep was about to reclaim me, I became even more convinced I could hear somebody moving about.

I tiptoed down the stairs feeling a mixture of terror and outrage. Of course I should have dialed 999, or called Inspector Flowers direct, without delay. It did cross my mind that this might have something to do with the murder of Dennis, yet surely in a city of ten million people it was far more likely to be a complete coincidence, whereas break-ins were as common as branches of KFC, without Colonel Sanders serving. I hadn't even got Stan to turn to, hopeless though he might have been, but I crept determinedly on, my footsteps muffled by the shag pile carpet.

I could hear the intruder, still oblivious of me, continuing to rifle through the drawer in the study. However, I'd reclaimed the element of surprise from him. I reached for Stan's heavy-duty radio award with my right hand, ready to strike him if need be.

'You better give your heart to Jesus 'cos your butt is mine,' I said in true down-home style.

'Give me the formula,' he calmly replied. He was six foot tall, had mean murderous eyes and was waving a gun at me.

'I strongly advise you to leave my house now unless you want runner-up regional broadcaster of the year to come crashing down on your head,' I said.

'Give me the fucking formula!' he said with more intensity. Then in one swift move he lurched forward and pistol whipped me with his gun, propelling me to the ground while relieving me of Stan the Man's trophy and pinning me to the floor.

'You know what I've come for,' he hissed into my face.

I don't suppose a hefty kick in the balls was quite the answer he was expecting. It sure made him release his grip. As he lay there moaning, I made straight for his discarded gun and fired a warning shot at him – I was raised in Atlanta, Georgia for God's sake. I deliberately missed him by an inch.

'Mad fucking bitch!' he yelled at me.

'That's no way to speak to a lady, especially if she's aiming a smoking gun right at your cock. It's not a very big target, admittedly, but I was raised with guns, so unless you want to finish up as the rooster who became a hen I'd get the hell out of here.'

He took flight, and I fired another shot just above his head while he limped away like a stuck pig.

'Come back here again and it won't be just the force of my foot you'll be feeling between your legs!' I yelled like a crazy lady. 'Us southern girls shoot balls for fun where we come from – testicles make prizes!'

I didn't expect to be seeing that particular gentleman back here any time soon.

What with all that adrenalin pumping around me, I was now up for anything. A certain officer of the law crossed my mind. Need to get ravished, and want a mystery solving too? Who are you going to call? Inspector Flowers!

Although when the Inspector finally picked up he sounded tireder than a stump-tailed cow in fly time.

'Who is it?' he asked mechanically.

'It's me, Miss Caro. I really don't know whether I should be bothering you, but our home has just been broken into by an armed man searching for a formula.'

'Of course you were right to call. Any injury?'

'No, I only fired warning shots, but I sure as hell gave him a fright.'

'I was thinking more about you, Miss Kennedy,' he replied, 'but it seems like the guy had a lucky let off.' He was chuckling down the phone.

'Don't imagine I'm not all shook up though. I could call 999 if you would prefer it.'

'No, don't do that.' His tone was more serious. 'I'll be there just as soon as I can, and don't touch a thing.'

How lucky was I to have a hotline to such a hot cop. And no sooner had he entered the house than everything seemed OK again. I was delighted to greet my knight in shining armor. He was still wearing the same Paul Smith suit.

'Are you sure you're OK?' said the Inspector, eyeing me up and down. Was he looking for any signs of injury, or was it just a convenient excuse to check out my body? I so hoped so. 'Perhaps you need to get yourself checked out at hospital,' he suggested.

'No need – it's the other guy you should be worrying about. He left here like a scalded cat with his tail between his legs. He was lucky I didn't shoot it off him.'

'Just as well you didn't, we have laws against that kind of stuff in this country,' the Inspector said.

'I might look fine and dandy but in truth I'm kind of all over the place, Inspector,' I said. I touched him on his right arm. Yes, it was time to play the vulnerability card.

'I could fix you up with our victim support unit,' he kindly offered.

I pulled a face. 'I guess a nice hug would be out the question?'

Well, I was badly shaken up.

He was clearly a people person who put feelings above tedious rules and regulations, because his response was to smile and place his strong muscular arms around me. He held me for the briefest of moments, but it was long enough for me to know that I would have liked it to last a darn sight longer. I came that close to throwing myself on his mercy and ripping his shirt off. Surely his boss would understand, considering the stress I had just endured in my own home at the hands of a maniac?

While I suspected he had feelings for me, above all else Inspector Flowers was that kind of rare guy who is not ruled by his desires, only the wish to deliver a supremely professional service to the public. Or maybe I was losing my touch?

'Aren't you going to probe me?' I asked him suggestively. 'You must have so many questions you want to ask.'

'Later Miss Caro, after you've enjoyed some well-earned rest,' he said.

So, while I went to bed to try to get some shuteye, Inspector Flowers brought in forensics to examine the crime scene. He promised to be there for me when I woke up, to take a statement from me, or anything else he wanted. Needless to say, I felt safe in his hands.

CHAPTER FIVE

Early the next morning, Inspector Flowers awoke me with a cup of tea and two Garibaldi biscuits on a china plate. I was only too happy to have him all to myself, in my boudoir, a room for romance rather than sleeping.

'How kind of you Inspector,' I said, giving him a big smile. 'Have you and your team completed your investigations downstairs?'

'We have indeed – I've sent the guy from forensics home. It's just me now.' I patted the side of my bed for him to sit on. He was now only one short, sharp, decisive move away from getting into bed with me.

I begged him not to go public with this latest incident, not wanting Carla to bump me off any more shows, or to generate further lurid publicity.

'If you're certain that's what you really want. It will be our little secret,' he replied.

'Whatever you think is best, Inspector,' I said. 'And when you're not being an Inspector, what is it you like to do?'

'I'm pretty much devoted to my job, which takes up most of my time, but when I do get the occasional free moment I'm an enthusiastic reader. Not trashy stuff but great Literature, like Dickens and Hardy.'

'Ah, I'm more of a Margaret Mitchell girl myself, but when I need something more substantial I have been known to partake of a Dickens or a Hardy myself.'

'I don't doubt it,' he replied.

'Although I do prefer Dickens' longer ones. Maybe we could enjoy one together sometime.' I lay back on my pillow and adjusted my nightdress, not wanting to be the harlot to his cop. Well, look where it had got me with my hot next-door neighbor, only to become an abandoned, love-sick woman.

'If only I had time, with so much police work to do,' he replied, his dark eyes darting back and forth. That was quite enough literature, if that's what it was.

'And is there a Mrs Flowers at home, to mop your brow between cases?' I asked, having already looked at his left hand and failing to find any evidence.

'No, I don't think it would be fair. I wouldn't be able to give her the time she deserved, being always tied up with police work.'

'Come to think of it, you never read about Mrs Sherlock Holmes or a Madame Poirot. That could be why.'

'Much as I would love to talk to you for longer, I better get on – I've got cases to solve,' he said abruptly.

I hadn't intended him to get away that suddenly. 'You can't leave me, I'm still in a state of shock,' I said.

'I'll get on to victim support,' he assured me.

'I've never been a victim in my life, and I darn well refuse to become one now,' I replied.

'I didn't mean to upset you, it's just a police term. I could see if you qualify for a twenty-four-hour bodyguard, at least until we get a better idea of who broke into your house.'

'Only if it's you,' I couldn't help blurting out.

'That would be strictly against regulations.'

'Because I feel I know you, and I could trust you around the place.'

'I suppose there would be no harm in asking to see if they would consider it. But what about your male tenant – isn't he around?'

'He's away on a course on how to become a woman.'

'Now why doesn't that surprise me? It should.'

'Because you're an open minded, free thinking, man of the world, Inspector, although you'd have no chance of graduating if you were on Stan's course.'

'That's one exam I would be only too happy to fail,' he replied.

As he departed to make that call about becoming my minder he was looking somewhat discombobulated, probably a bit disturbed about what he'd got himself into. I could have kicked myself for being so forward. I really didn't want to frighten the poor man away.

When he returned to announce that they'd agreed for him to move in with me for an initial twenty-four-hour period, I was already contemplating what it would be like to become a policeman's wife. Presumptuous or what?

'It's just a temporary arrangement,' he explained when I joined him downstairs for tea and cakes.

'Well, ain't that the berries,' I said. He looked confused.

'Don't worry – people struggle to understand what the hell I'm talking about in New York, so lord only knows what they make of me in London. I'm speaking southern you see, from the deep south of the USA. I don't always need to speak like this – it's my security blanket for when the going gets tough. It reconnects me with home.'

'Is that what it is? I find it charming.'

I can do charming, and flighty, not to mention flirty. It all comes in useful on my late night radio show. So just you and me then?'

'It seems like it – if that's OK with you?'

'We could play a game of Scrabble, except you'd be scoring high on a triple word with that Dickens of yours'.

'Proper names are not allowed,' he said, and then he left to collect his overnight bag. I did hope I hadn't overdone it. I reckon he was beginning to regret ever mentioning his passion for Victorian classics.

While he was gone I started fretting about what to wear for him – the sultry little number that always got guys going in next to no time, or the stylish slow-burner that lured them in subtly and then preyed on their senses until they could think of nothing else. But none of this would happen by magic - I really needed to get into shape, not only for Inspector Flowers but for the viewing millions who would be checking me out on Capital TV. Still I regretted this backward step in my career, although my feelings were obviously tempered by the eyewatering amounts of money that had enticed me back to revealing more of my self than might be considered seemly, for commercial gain.

I didn't even need to move out of my luxurious Hampstead lodgings any more, not now that Stan had gone all transgender. I mean really, what more could the poor boy to do to prove his lack of interest in me than to change sex? I had no need to worry about Stan, now that he'd found himself, and I felt so much more secure with Inspector Flowers around the place – a real man at my beck and call. I even called my mom and dad back home in Atlanta to let them know I had my own personal security. I was glad to put their minds at rest regarding my safety, as bad news travels far and fast. Not that I could talk to them for too long, as I had to link up with my esteemed new personal trainer, Darnell, who put me through my paces unexpectedly aggressively for a first session, although it made his full body massage afterwards all the more agreeable. What's not to like about being manipulated by a super fit, six-foot tall, ebony athlete?

And how lovely to arrive home to find my very own bodyguard preparing food in the kitchen.

'Making yourself at home, I see, Inspector Flowers.'

'I do hope that's OK. I thought I'd rustle up my signature dish, spag bol, for us, if that's OK?'

'My, that would be fine. I wasn't expecting catering as well as bodyguarding.'

'It's all part of the package,' said the Inspector. That shouldn't have got me wondering whether his package might be part of the package too. I was feeling too rampant for my own good. Anyway, the meal was mighty fine, and what's lovelier than being cooked for and waited on hand and foot by a truly handsome man?

That evening Inspector Flowers accompanied me to Capital Talk, where I so wanted to impress him with my intellect and ability to connect with the Great British Public. I could tell he wasn't the type of guy to be put off by a woman having a career – on the contrary, I thought he would relish it. I would prove to him that I was much more than a curvaceous, five-foot-nine blonde who could occasionally turn a guy's head.

Rather predictably, Tom gave him a welcome straight out of the freezer, demanding to see his ID – since when had Tom become a security expert? – before ordering him to sit in the green room, and not in the studio with us, in their battle to see who should be crowned the true alpha male. So predictable, but I'd be putting all my money on Flowers.

'I insist on sitting within the vicinity of Miss Kennedy so that I can intervene should she be in any danger,' he told Tom good and proper. I reckoned I was going to win my bet, as Tom reluctantly backed down.

'Play nicely, boys,' I instructed them, after Tom had gracelessly ordered Flowers 'to keep his mouth shut,' and not to intervene in the show. 'You only get to watch,' Tom told him, which sounded slightly pervy. I'd never have guessed he was so insecure. He wasn't at all pleased that I'd chosen a serious political subject to kick off the show either – should failing to vote in a General Election be made illegal? – saying it would wreck our ratings.

'I think it's voting which should be made illegal, it only encourages them,' said Gerald from Ponders Green, a well-worn cliché I'd heard plenty of times before.

'So, you don't believe in democracy, Gerald,' I said, clenching my fist and blowing on my fingernails in a gesture which said 'follow that loser'.

'Who wins elections is entirely irrelevant. And do you know why?'

'I have this funny feeling you're going to tell us, Gerald,' I said with just the slightest trace of sarcasm evident in my voice.

'Governments control squiddly diddly. The real power lies in the hands of the corporations and the shadowy figures, once referred to by Her Majesty the Queen when she let it slip, who operate under the cover of our so-called democratic institutions.'

I really didn't want an intelligent man like Inspector Flowers to be subjected to such crapola, fearing it might reflect badly on me. My heart sank faster than a raccoon falling out of a deadwood tree. How was I expected to impress a well-read man like the good Inspector with callers like these?

It was almost a relief to be interrupted by a news flash from our newsroom announcing that Iran had just tested another inter-continental ballistic missile – not that getting Gerald off the airwaves was worth starting World War Three for, although it was a close-run thing.

What a relief to speak to our next caller, Steph from Wimbledon – the clue was in the name. Women are so much less likely to be conspiracy obsessives, except about the death of Princess Diana.

'Talking of elections, Miss Caro, do you think that Emmanuel Macron, the President of France, is hot? And he's twenty-five-years younger than his wife, lucky cow. How does that happen?'

'OK, so when you see him standing next to President Trump, sure he looks hot – doesn't everybody? But I am more kindly disposed towards a bigger, more manly man,' I said, looking Inspector Flowers straight in the eye.

'I'm more drawn to power, and women being entertained by younger fitter guys,' said Steph.

'I'll vote for that too, Miss Steph. And when you see him and his much older wife on TV together, they look like they're still doing it, even though she's 64 and he's 39.' I hoped Inspector Flowers would be suitably impressed by that particular piece of knowledge – what a mine of information, he must be thinking, or was he nodding off?

'Macron's always got a twinkle in his eye,' said Steph.

'Isn't that a euphemism for something else? We're supposed to be talking elections, not erections,' Tom rudely interrupted – not big or clever at all. I doubt that Inspector Flowers would be the least bit impressed.

'So, who's your ideal man, Miss Caro?' Steph asked.

I wanted to reply, he's this hot Police Inspector who's sitting right next to me. And then it struck me that ever since Inspector Flowers had figured in my life I hadn't been yearning after Larry, for the first time in absolutely ages.

'I have to confess to liking something a little more super macho than Macron,' I explained. 'How about Idris Elba? He's man enough for both of us.'

'Where would you ever hope to find a guy like that?' said Steph forlornly.

'Oh, I don't know,' I replied teasingly, winking at the good Inspector. Had I taken leave of my senses?

'I have to admit, Steph,' said Tom, butting in – who asked him? – 'I do reckon it's kind of sexy the idea of

18-year-old Macron copping off with his 43-year-old teacher. Every schoolboy's dream, because what's not to like about a MILF? But as for a 64-year-old woman getting it on with a 39-year man – well, it's not natural, is it?'

'Once again, Tom has proved that he's a complete male dinosaur, unable to accept that their relationship could be anything other than an adolescent school boy's fantasy, and not a real grown-up lifelong partnership.'

'I hope I can still pull a 39-year-old guy when I'm 64,' said Steph.

'Why shouldn't you, Miss Steph? It's the way of the future, for all of us women. It's the age of the female,' I proudly pronounced before we swung into another commercial break. And this from a woman who preferred older men. If our show was about anything, it was about variety, from Steph highlighting the question of whether an older woman and a younger man could be a great idea to Olaf, our Polish trucker, who claimed that he felt he was no longer welcome in the UK following our departure from the European Union.

'Everybody used to be my friend, now they say, it's time for you to go home, Olaf,' said Olaf. 'And I say, this is home, and they say back, not any more, Polskie boy.'

'Well, we love having you here on Capital Talk, whatever those idiots say.'

'And I love you Miss Caro, and wherever I am in the world in my truck, you are always with me.'

'Praise the Lordy for digital radio, eh?'

'And praises for my sexy photo of you in basque and suspenders, stroking a big gun – it will always be number one pin-up in my cab.'

'Send me a copy, can you?' Tom rudely interrupted. I covered my face in shame. That was something I had done for the army on Salisbury Plain, if my memory serves me right. It was all about raising morale, according to the fit young captain who persuaded me against my better judgement to do it (although I never turn down a request from the military). Now what was his name? – ah yes, Harry Windsor. It wasn't until later that I found out he was some kind of Prince. I'd only been dining with Prince Harry, while all I still cared about was my Larry. It could have been Harry and Miss Caro, not Meghan and the Prince, if I'd played my cards right, and it would have been me who had her hands on the Crown Jewels, not her. Or maybe I was overestimating myself. However, I will never forget his ticklish beard during the passionate kiss he unexpectedly gave me on the lips on leaving his barracks, as he thanked me for raising the morale of his troops – including his, if my eyes didn't deceive me. Still, it's nice to see a good, wholesome American girl like Meghan by his side, as I often said through gritted teeth.

Of course, I was so glad to hear of Harry settling down. If only I could have been as lucky as them with my Larry.

Still, back at Capital Towers I had to hand over to

Stan's stand-in, known as the Fox, who fancied himself as some kind of new age Barry White, with his deep-voiced delivery, although he came from the Isle of Dogs. On came the backing track to *Never Going To Give You Up*, to trail his raunchy new show, where he would encourage listeners to phone in about their favourite positions under the guise of sex therapy, wanting me to join in his various moans and sighs – as if I would do such a thing, at least not in front of Inspector Flowers, who had slipped out, no doubt on important police business.

'I can give you more than you ever thought possible, Miss Caro,' he purred to me through the microphone, with the track still playing in the backgound.

'But good sir, I'm not that kind of gal, and why, I was once betrothed to Stan the Man, in whose chair you currently sit,' I replied in my finest Southern.

'Every girl is that kind of girl when she goes hunting with the Fox. And I can give you more than Stan ever could'.

'I don't doubt it. A woman has needs too, and mine soooooo need to be met.' I trailed off into a couple of Donna Summer-style moans, while the voice-over man trailed the next episode of our on-air affair the following night.

What with my southern belle tones and the Fox's basso profundo naughtiness we were guaranteed to get London playing with itself, to quote Carla's delightful turn of phrase. But I had higher aspirations than that, as

I constantly reminded my ratings hungry boss.

When I touched base with Inspector Flowers again, was it my imagination or was he looking at me in a whole different way, like I was some kind of media whore?

'That was different,' he said.

Talk about being damned with faint praise.

But he eventually claimed to have enjoyed the majority of the show, in the way that a highly-educated guy would if he was pretending to like it against his better judgement.

'You really have to think on your feet while making it look easy,' he said by way of congratulating me.

Who cared if it wasn't his particular bowl of grits, because he'd be the one driving me home tonight, and hanging out in the room just across the landing when we got back there. I was going all tingly at just the thought of it.

'So, you won't be needing a ride in my car?' said Tom, trying to stir it up.

'As if, Tom. Not when a gal's got a professional bodyguard like the Inspector here to look after her. I couldn't be in better hands.' I smiled at him cruelly. That would show him.

There would be no placing a blue light on top of the car and driving me back at breakneck speed, given the lateness of the hour, the Inspector explained. Instead we would ride in his comfortable Mercedes at a nice leisurely pace, getting to know each other as we went.

'Your callers obviously love you,' he said.

'And I love them too. You start to develop a bond, even with some of the conspiracy nutters. After all, they're probably just lonely, wanting somebody to talk to.'

'But it's more than that – it's like they depend on you as somebody who can help them get through the night, and they'd be lost without you,' he kindly observed.

I couldn't help but be flattered by his compliments. I was so glad that he really got it, and didn't look down on my little show.

'I know this might sound stupid, Inspector Flowers, but I genuinely care about my listeners, in a way that you do with friends, wanting to help and encourage them whenever I can, and to try and get back on track when they're obviously losing it,' I said.

He made a sharp turn left. 'That's because you're a kind person, Miss Kennedy, getting them through those difficult night-time hours so they never have to be on their own, because their good friend Miss Caro is available at the flick of a switch.'

What a kind and gracious Inspector he was.

'And I really appreciate what you're doing for me, Inspector, especially as you've bent the rules to make it happen.'

'Don't even mention it,' he said.

I sat back in the Merc, reclining on its luxurious seats. He had to be highly thought of, being permitted a vehicle like this. I was thinking seriously about what I had become, and how my show was in danger of getting trashier by the hour.

'I tell you what, I'm refusing to do that handover to The Fox, however much Carla believes it helps to boost our ratings,' I said. 'She claims that literally thousands of people are setting their alarms to see what happens next between us, and they won't be happy until we finish up doing it on the desk. What's wrong with people?'

'I'm sorry I missed it,' said the Inspector, crossing a junction on amber. Police inspectors are permitted to do stuff like that.

'Anyway, Stan will be back soon, and I certainly won't be doing any erotic moaning with him.'

I must admit, I do find it hard to believe you were ever engaged to him.'

'Then you don't understand women, Inspector Flowers. A girl falls head over heels in love with a guy, ignoring all rational evidence to the contrary, even when she knows he's a control freak who's slowly going to wear her down, while neglecting her in bed, making her feel unattractive. Everyone around you tells you, Miss Caro, he's not right for you, but still you don't see it, because you're intoxicated by love. That was until Larry came along – but then he went and dumped me too.'

I'm sure the good Inspector didn't need to know all this, and it was most unlikely to be putting him in the mood for *lurve*. What kind of aphrodisiac would that be? But I just couldn't stop unburdening myself. I was incorrigible.

'You don't seem to be very lucky with men,' he rightly observed.

'Or maybe they get lucky with me, by getting out in time.'

'You're being too hard on yourself.'

'Just listen to me going on like this, it's as if you're an agony aunt, not a po-leece inspector.'

'It's all part of the job,' he replied. I'd rather hoped it might be something even more personal. How stupid was I?

When we got to my place the last thing I needed was any further shocks to the system, considering the fragile state I was in, but that's what I got.

'I don't want to worry you Miss Caro, but I fear you might have an unwelcome guest hiding in your doorway,' he said calmly.

'Oh Lordy, not another one!' I cried out loud. But he was right. Crouching in the doorway was a figure with a ludicrously grotesque face that wouldn't have looked out of place on a gargoyle. I thanked my lucky stars that my officer friend was on hand to deal with it. Without a moment's hesitation or any thought for his own safety, he threw open the car door and gave chase. The creature ran off, swinging its arms from side to side as it went. The Inspector wasn't far behind him and it would only have been a matter of time before he'd caught him, if he hadn't tripped in a pothole and come crashing down to the ground.

I ran to tend him, asking him where he'd been hurt.

'I don't appear to have broken anything. I'm so sorry to have let you down, Caro,' he said.

'But you haven't. Without you, God knows what would have happened,' I said. I can't deny that my confidence had taken a bit of a battering – one intruder I could deal with, but with two I was getting perilously out of my depth.

'OK, you'd better show me where I'm going to sleep' he said as we entered.

Well I wasn't having that. 'No way am I sleeping on my own tonight, you're coming in with me,' I said.

'I'm not sure my superiors at the Yard would approve,' he said.

'What they don't see won't hurt them. You're sleeping in my bed, and there's an end to it. We'll go head to toe – our heads at different ends of the bed, like when we were kids. What's the worst that could happen?'

In the end he agreed, but reluctantly. That wasn't great for my self-esteem, I can tell you.

We cracked open a bottle of vodka and downed so many glasses of the white stuff that I'm not sure we'd have noticed a herd of elephants if they'd popped in for buns. He claimed not to be a drinker, which is perhaps why he got sloshed so darn quickly. I usually prefer a man who can hold his liquor.

And so to bed, him at one end of the mattress and me at the other, both totally spaced out. There was no embarrassment at all, just a little bit of giggling on my part as he stripped down to his vest and underpants. I slipped into my nightdress in the bathroom before getting into bed to find him already fast asleep. Some bodyguard he was. It didn't take long for me to crash out either.

Now don't ask me how it happened, but when I awoke he was right there alongside me, same way up, strictly in contravention of the top-to-toe rule, and whoops, somehow my arms had got themselves wrapped around his manly torso. I can't deny that I felt the urge to explore him further, but instead I nodded off again and enjoyed an erotic dream in which I stole his handcuffs to tether him to my bed, do I could do whatever took my fancy. There sure was some fun to be had.

Having taken my fill of him, I suddenly realized that in all the excitement I'd mislaid the key to his cuffs. You should have seen the panic on his face, not to mention the shame when one of his colleagues had to be despatched to release him from his unfortunate predicament.

My relief on waking up to realize it was only a dream was somewhat tempered by discovering that my right hand was resting on his semi-erect cock. How the Dickens had it got there? And then I felt it start to grow... better not move it now... oh heavens, now what was I supposed to do? Where's the etiquette book that can advise a well-brought-up young Southern lady how to behave when she wakes up to find her hand on a gentleman's manhood?

Should she give him an encouraging hand, or get up and fix them both a nice cup of tea?

While I was deliberating, that thing of his just kept right on growing. Soon it was as pleasing a ding-a-ling as a young lady could ever hope to set eyes on.

'Time to get up,' I said on my return with teacups in hand, having made my difficult decision to err on the side of propriety. He was consulting his smartphone, from which he told me he had learned that the creature in the night had already been apprehended. He was just some hobo who'd been warned about trespassing on my property.

'I guess that's good news,' I said, but my heart sank, because now I knew there was no longer any need for him to stay around and guard my body. I'd missed my chance once more, and I suspected that I'd never see Inspector Flowers again.

Under the circumstances, it wasn't much consolation to know that Stan would be home soon, although at least I would have somebody to talk to. I was pleasantly surprised when I finally got to meet the new him – or should I say her? The course tutors had done a great job of transforming him from geeky guy to gorgeous girl. He was beginning to think like a woman too, allowing the female which must have been lying dormant for so long to surface. Stan was no more, and I was glad of it.

'You look fabulous, babe,' I told her. I loved her beautifully coordinated outfit of wide leg cropped pants with a bright red thin knit top and clean white boots. Her make-up was no less convincing, and nicely understated.

'That means so much, coming from you,' she said, like my opinion actually meant something.

'And what are we supposed to call you? I can't continue with Stan The Man.'

He explained that he'd been considering Anthea – no, me neither, too much the drag queen, if she wanted to be taken seriously as a girl.

The radio was on and Elkie Brooks was singing in the background. 'Pearl's a singer...'

'What about Pearl? Pearl the Girl? By Jove she's got it!' I proclaimed, like the guy in *My Fair Lady*. Stan hesitated at first, saying she would need time to see if she could live with it, but once I'd announced, 'Goodbye Stan the Man, hello Pearl the Girl,' there could be no going back, whether she liked it or not. And I reckoned she was pretty darn taken with it anyway – well who wouldn't be? A little old-fashioned maybe, but somehow so right for a girl like Stan. She would grow into it, once she'd let it all come out.

'But it's not all about me – what's been happening while I've been away?' enquired Stan, sorry Pearl.

'Oh, nothing much. Inspector Flowers moved in for a night after we'd been burgled, so I insisted we slept together after I'd been traumatized by this really weird-looking guy who showed up on our doorstep. So, we agreed to sleep head to toe, and then I somehow contrive to wake up with my hand on his impressive and still-growing cock. Now, what's a girl sp'osed to do, Miss Pearl?'

'It would be rude not to,' she suggested.

'Miss Pearl!' I exclaimed. 'I can see we're going to have to rein you in. And heaven only knows what he was dreaming about. You can bet it wasn't me!'

'Don't underestimate yourself,' she sweetly replied.

'So, I got up, got dressed, and made the Inspector a nice cup of tea – and I haven't seen him since.'

'Maybe you put too many sugars in his drink,' Pearl surmised. We both cracked up laughing at the whole ridiculous business of how to engage with men.

Regardless of Inspector Flowers, I was liking my new girlfriend more than I could have guessed. I suspected that Pearl would occupy an important place in my heart for years to come.

CHAPTER SIX

Pearl waited until the next day before telling me she had received a text from Carla firing her from her show on Capital Talk. Sometimes I wondered about my so-called best friend, Carla.

'Honey, how could she do that to you?' I yelled.

'It was all about ratings,' Pearl replied. 'Apparently the Fox has doubled the figures overnight, and I hear your handover to him has become quite a phenomenon.'

Boy, did I feel bad about that particular bowl of grits, seeing as how I'd laid it on thick at Stan's expense. But he wasn't Stan any more was he? He was Pearl.

I still gave Carla a piece of my mind. I burst into her office to have it out with her face to face.

'I didn't tell you because it would have put you in

an invidious position,' she said. Management speak for 'I was going to do it anyway'. 'He's become so predictable, Caro, with that same old woman-hating rhetoric.'

'Not any more he ain't, and you're gonna have to stop calling him Stan, because Stan is no more. From now on it's Pearl. You could have had the first transgender night time host on British Radio if you'd just waited a little bit longer.'

It took quite a lot to surprise Carla.

'Well who'd have thought it? So what does he, sorry she, look like?' she asked, as always cutting to the chase.

'Surprisingly good. In fact she's a darn site more convincing as a woman than she ever was as a man – and I should know, I nearly married him.'

'Bless him,' Carla observed. 'To think he was only a twin set and pearls away from becoming a proper human being.'

'So you'll re-hire her then? Or should I say hire Pearl to replace him?'

'I wouldn't go that far. Let's see how she gets on with her transgendering, and if she makes good progress, then I might be willing to consider it.'

At least I had a message of hope to deliver back to Pearl. A girl's got to have a career, hasn't she?

Having got business out of the way, Carla and I were able to revert to being friends again, although it could be a difficult tightrope to walk. I told her about my night of acute embarrassment with Inspector Flowers.

'So you had your hand resting on his awesome thingamajig and still you couldn't do the deed. You don't think you might be turning lesbian, do you? I'd be more than happy to give you a few notes.'

'No, you're OK. One woman's enough for any relationship, much as I love our gender.'

'Deep down, I reckon it was the memory of Larry that stopped you. He's like a ghost who refuses to stop haunting you. You really need to lay him to rest.'

'I sp'ose I do.'

'Do you know what, Caro? You need to revisit your past, and ask him exactly why he finished with you – to find closure, as you Americans like to call it, and then maybe you'll be able to move on. Besides, he's probably grey, fat and ugly by now, and if that doesn't put you off, nothing will.'

'You might be right, darn you. Aren't you always?'

'And I could give you some time off to sort yourself out.'

'That's probably because you want to fire me and hire my stand-in.'

'You're much too hot a property to let go, especially with your upcoming exposure on Capital TV.'

'Thanks for reminding me,' I said, still totally underwhelmed by my return to the ranks of weather girl, the job I was about to start later that day.

Sure, I was greeted most kindly at the TV studios by Charlene, the Australian producer there, who promised she'd make it as painless as possible, but then blew it all by explaining that I'd be required to film a series of catwalk sequences wearing different styles of lingerie – all very tasteful, Victoria's Secret of course, but my heart wasn't really in it. That was until she informed me that Prince Harry and Prince William were big fans of the brand and could well be tuning in. That would give me the necessary oomph as I worked it just for them.

On the way out there was the usual bunch of autograph hunters you see standing outside theatres and TV studios in their anoraks, lining up for me to write my name in their books and assorted scraps of paper, and out of politeness, I always used to oblige them.

'Great to see you back on TV,' said one of them while I was writing. I could kind of guess why he was thankful for my return, and I don't think isobars and long-range forecasts would rank highly among his reasons.

'Hope I can bring you plenty of relief over the next few weeks – and that's a type of rainfall, just in case you were wondering,' I said to him. I swear he nearly passed out. And it wasn't just him - there were 50 more shades of anoraks lined up for me to pose with on their phones.

'Smile girlfriend,' I said to another who reminded me of Stan before his transformation, with his smooth hairless cheeks. And he didn't seem to be at all upset by my questioning his masculinity. In fact, he positively relished it. There must be something in the water, perhaps all those hormones which have been turning male fish female.

But then the next guy came along, and he was a totally different kettle of catfish. He was about the same age as the others but he had a strikingly different demeanor about him compared with the more challenged guys further up the line.

'I'll need a piece of paper and a pen if you want an autograph,' I explained to him.

'Thanks for offering Miss Caro, but that's not why I'm here,' he said nonchalantly. 'I was wondering if you'd like to accompany me for tea at the Ritz?' He sounded almost as posh as a real Royal, like my friend Prince Harry, although much younger of course.

He might have turned a young girl's head, with his dark, moody eyes and smooth, light brown skin, although I doubted if he was anywhere close to buying booze legally. Whatever, it was a totally ridiculous notion for me to take tea with this boy at the Ritz – with me, who preferred older, more worldly, macho men - just the thought of it made me want to laugh out loud.

'Sure,' I said nonchalantly back. My reply took even me by surprise. OK, so, he had a lovely deep voice for one so young, and you could tell that he'd been working out, with those strong arms of his and a wide expansive chest and surprisingly muscular thighs. But what was I even thinking of sizing up a teenage boy like this, me the connoisseur of the hot, sophisticated older gentleman?

Maybe all that modelling of sexy lingerie while thinking of Prince Harry had got me rampant. Best I make an excuse and get the hell out of there.

'Oh, do you know what?' I said, 'I've just remembered that I have to meet a journalist from the Evening Standard who wants to interview me about what I'll be wearing for the Royal Wedding.'

'Make them wait,' he replied. And I succumbed to him again, as if he had some kind of power over me. It looked like I was on my way to the Ritz with an adolescent boy who couldn't be bothered to collect autographs when he could collect the person instead.

'Can we come too?' said one of the poor loser boys.

'You can fuck off,' he said to them, echoing my own sentiments, although I would never have phrased it quite like that. I doubt any of those poor boys had even taken a girl out to McDonalds, let alone the Ritz, bless their little cotton Y Fronts, whereas this new guy had real class, way beyond his years. I bet he wore Calvin Kleins. Even the taxis we lining up for him. Every driver seemed to want to be his fare.

'Do you mind me asking, how old are you?' I enquired once we got moving and were seated next to one another on the back seat of the cab.

'You haven't got to worry – I'm legal, if that's what you're worried about,' he replied with an audacious smile.

'You don't think you might be getting a bit above yourself?' I said, although I couldn't help but be intrigued by him.

'I didn't mean to presume,' he said, backtracking like crazy. 'I just didn't want you to feel uncomfortable around me.' That was more like it. 'But should you be interested, I'm 17 going on 18,' he added.

'Just like Ralph in the Sound of Music. It's one of my favorite films.'

'I can't say I've seen it.'

'Now that's what I call a generation gap – although it's far too old for me too, really.'

You should have seen the way he swanned into The Ritz, like he owned the place – or maybe his parents did.

'A table in the name of Potter?' he demanded of the haughty-looking waiter, who immediately submitted to the will of this super-confident young man.

'Certainly sir. We've reserved you the best table in the house, overlooking Piccadilly Circus.'

'Wow, there's confidence,' I said once the waiter was out of range. 'You'd already booked a table for two, even before I said yes to your invitation. What would you have done if I'd turned you down?'

'Unlikely, but I'd have cancelled, of course.'

He had an answer for everything, although I could have done without the 'of course'.

Then the waiter returned, treating him with so much respect that this kid must not only have been on first name terms with the princes, but the Queen too. 'Reception have asked me to inform you that your room will be ready once tea has been served, Mr Potter.'

You could have heard a cucumber sandwich drop, such was my amazement. 'There's being over-confident, and there's being downright presumptuous,' I said, packing away my stuff, 'and you've just crossed the line.'

For the first time I glimpsed a trace of panic in the boy's eyes, as if he was losing control.

'I really don't know what to say, Miss Caro,' he said. He was probably planning to kill that waiter later. 'It's just that when I'm out with a lady, people are always saying 'get a room,' so I did.'

'I hope you'll be very happy in it alone, Mr Potter,' I said, preparing to make a rapid but elegant exit.

'Please don't go,' he begged. 'I've waited for this moment ever since I first started listening to your show on Jolly Roger FM.'

'You should have thought of that earlier,' I said.

'But I'm only 17 going on 18, with so much to learn,' he pleaded with me.

It was like The Sound Of Music all over again, even if I was more of Captain Von Trapp kind of girl. How could I not be touched by his plea?

'And I totally love Into The Night. I feel as though I already know you, listening to you every night alone in my bed at public school. I hate conspiracy theories too. And to be sitting here with you for real – I think it must have all gone to my head.'

Suddenly I felt compelled to give the boy a second chance.

'So, why aren't you out enjoying having tea with girls of your own age?' I said, taking my seat again.

'You really want to know? They bore me,' he said, returning to his old, confident self. 'Of course, I've dated teenage girls, but once you've had dealings, what is there to talk about, unless it's Harry Style's latest haircut, or which shade of lipstick suits Cheryl Cole best. Whereas when I first heard you on Into The Night putting those idiots to rights about the latest nonsense they'd picked up from the net, I knew I'd found the one.'

I couldn't help but feel humbled by his words. What girl wouldn't?

'Although I can't deny I also enjoyed reading your good bikini guide in the Sunday People Magazine. I've got it on my bedroom wall at school,' said Mr Potter.

'Why wouldn't you?' I said, smiling flirtatiously and allowing him to have his happy moment.

'Oh God, you so know how to fill a bikini,' he sighed.

'More tea, Mr Potter?' I asked, trying to change the conversation to something more refined. But he was unrelenting as he took another sip of his Earl Grey.

'I can tell you what you're thinking, that I'm too young for you, but I can assure you that I'm not without experience in affairs of the heart with ladies of more mature years, and most of them far older than you.'

I wasn't sure where this was going, but I would be glad when it got there.

'So who were these ladies?' I just had to ask.

'Three of them were friends of my mother. She never knew of course, and I never had any complaints from any of them.'

'Too much information, Mr Potter. What would your mom say if she ever found out?'

'She'd probably thank them for getting me up and running once she'd had a good shout at them and lambasted me.'

'Let it be known, I'm not that old. I'm not even thirty yet,' I forcefully reminded him.

'Precisely, which is why we should be together,' he argued, as if it was the most obvious thing in the world.

'And I won't let you down, because I'm through with playing around – I've already sown all my wild oats, so now I'm ready to settle down,' he said, as unlikely a thing as you would ever hear from a 17-year-old boy.

'So, if we're planning to settle down I sp'ose I should know your first name by now?' The panic in his eyes returned. 'Come on – out with it,' I urged him. Was it going to be one of those ridiculous British upper-class names like Benedict or Tarquin?

'It's Barry,' he confessed. 'My dad was posted to Kenya, and apparently it's a cool name out there.' Suddenly I started to put one and one together. 'And before you start, I was born before JK Rowling even got published. You can only imagine the grief I get, like, anybody for Quidditch, or how are things with Voldemort.'

'Barry Potter!' I cried out loud. But he was so unlike

his near namesake, being in no way geeky, without the NHS glasses, and with that lightly muscular athletic body.

'Pleased to meet you,' I said, shaking his hand.

And then as I contemplated those friends of his mom losing their respectability by making whoopee with him, it suddenly became understandable to me, if not right.

The next thing I knew, I was making my way to his room. Well, I'd never seen inside one of their ritzy rooms before. I guess he must have assumed he'd won me over, although that couldn't be further from the truth. It was a simple matter of curiosity.

Of course, the room was beautifully appointed, as you would expect of the Ritz, with a classic four-poster bed. And while I do confess to admiring Barry Potter for his sheer cheek there was no way I was falling for his plan.

'Thank you so much for the guided tour Barry, but I ought to be going.'

'But why?' he said, incomprehension written all over his face.

'Because I don't want to be the one who steals your youth. It's too great a responsibility.'

'I already told you – my youth has long since gone.'

'Ah yes, those MILFS of yours. But I'm not in the habit of being picked up and going to bed with a teenager I hardly know.'

'Then we could meet again for tea, or maybe dinner some time? I would never want to rush you,' he begged.

'You're going to make some girl very happy, Barry Potter, but it's not going to be me,' I said.

'Couldn't I at least kiss you goodbye?'

'I'm not sure that's wise,' I said, hesitating. He looked so forlorn. 'Go on then,' I replied.

I had never guessed what an exquisite kisser he would be. After he'd given me a peck on the cheek, we stood there for a short while, my cue to go, I guess, which I ignored. That emboldened him to kiss me full on the lips, and I responded in kind, until I came to my senses and pulled back from him, knowing that what we were doing was plain wrong. Then I felt his strong arms around me as he moved his entire body towards mine, our two ardent bodies locked together by forbidden passion.

'I do declare,' I said as I came up for air. 'Is that a magic wand in your pocket, Barry Potter, or are you just pleased to see me?'

But I didn't give him a chance to reply. I slipped away while I still could and headed back home to prepare for that evening's show. Sometimes, a girl has got to do the right thing – and let him find love with somebody much nearer to his own age. I couldn't resist the joke, though.

CHAPTER SEVEN

It took me longer than expected to get Barry Potter out of my head, as if he'd cast one of his Hogwarty spells on me. Maybe I was disturbed by having feelings for him, which was surely wrong, if not downright sinful, considering I was old enough to know better. But as Pearl rightly reminded me, there was only an eleven-year age gap between Barry and me, and if it was the other way around, it would seem totally fine and dandy.

'If it helps cure you of Larry, then why not go with it?' Pearl advised.

Then what was I supposed to do? Visit every English public school in the country to find out where my toyboy was hanging out? I would very soon have the law on my tail. Anyway, I much preferred older men. But not all problems came dressed up as men – Pearl's were of a financial nature. What with losing her job, and an ill-advised investment in a local radio franchise, it looked like she was going to have to sell the house.

'You'll need to find a new landlady, Miss Caro. I'll so miss living with you,' she said. Just then a great idea came to me, like a raccoon had fallen out of a magnolia tree onto my head.

'Why don't I buy the house from you?' I suggested. 'Then you can go on living here as my tenant, at a very affordable rent – like no rent at all. At least until Carla relents and takes you back to Capital Talk.'

'Can you afford it?' she asked.

'After that ridiculous new contract? I should darn well say so,' I replied.

I opened a bottle of cava to cement our new living arrangements, and to celebrate becoming a woman of property. Then I promised to finance both her hair removal and hormone therapy treatment, just the first of a series of feminizing procedures she would undergo before going the full transgender, if that's what she ultimately decided to do.

Why wouldn't I want to help? If we were to go out on the town together, I wanted her looking her very best, as I knew she would for the forthcoming variety show, or vaudeville as we call it in the States, at the Hackney Empire Theatre. Mind you, I can't say I always quite got British humor – apart from those old Carry On films, which usually featured some busty young wench stuck with an ineffectual boyfriend until real man Sid James popped up to put the smile back on her face. Story of my life really, Larry having become my Sid.

So, we would launch Pearl's new life as a woman at the after-show party, when a whole bunch of celebrities were expected to show up. Rather weirdly, I was now considered to be one of them – not because of my acclaimed radio phone-in show but because of flaunting myself in lingerie on Capital TV while telling them whether it was going to stay fine for their barbecues at the weekend. I had made my bed!

More crucially, Pearl looked so cute in her little black dress that I was proud to have her by my side on the red carpet. 'If only your mommy could see you now,' I said, teasing him. 'She'll certainly have a shock when she sees you in tomorrow's papers.'

Of course, she would blame it all on me, as was her way during our engagement when we had lived together.

The night of the show came, and those of us designated as celebrities, and our friends, were ushered towards the front row of the theatre.

'Great view,' said Pearl.

'It's so the host can pick on us,' I explained, just as a rather slimy stand-up comedian started engaging us in banter – or should that be humiliation – after he'd introduced each one of us to the audience. 'Caroline

Kennedy, ladies and gentlemen,' he said, inviting the audience to applaud. 'The weather girl who's infamous for getting us all hot and bothered even when it's freezing cold.'

I smiled graciously and did that thing with my forefinger where you pretend to touch something hot and make a *psssssst* noise and recoil from the heat.

'So, tell me Miss Caro, how do you work out what the weather is going to be like?' he asked, giving a conspiratorial wink to the audience – their permission for them to laugh at my expense. 'Do you use stuff like satellite charts and computers, or are you more a seaweed kind of girl, or do you just read what they've written for you on autocue?'

There were sniggers of cynical laughter.

'Certainly not the first two,' I replied, acting as if I'd been put firmly in my place. 'I use the same skill that enables me to tell how big a guy's dick is without getting his pants off.' That got the audience laughing at him, and he grinned painfully, shuffling uncomfortably on his feet and waiting for me to deliver the killer line.

'And looking at you, if I caught a catfish that small, I'd have to throw it back.' That brought a roar of approval, mostly from the ladies. That would teach him to question my weather forecasting skills.

He had nowhere to go but to introduce the first act, a fire-eater on a unicycle from Brazil, followed by a lady harpist from the Isle of Man, then on to the hilarious comedian Tim Vine, who cracked pithy one-liners, and then the singer Tony Christie, who sang a song about needing to know the way to Amarillo – as if anybody in their right mind would want to go there.

Then, topping the bill, we were invited to welcome on stage Mr Know All, the human search engine. 'So, what would you like to know?' he asked the audience. 'And I don't do football,' he added, which came as a relief to the majority of us.

'Name the Arsenal Invincibles who won the Premier League in 2002,' the breakfast TV presenter Piers Morgan annoyingly asked, as if just to wind him up.

'Give me three fascinating facts about my home town of Atlanta,' I challenged him, just to get over the embarrassment caused by Piers.

'Atlanta is the capital of the US State of Georgia, but it's the fifth city to be given that accolade,' he correctly answered. 'Almost all directions in Atlanta include the phrase 'go down Peach Tree,' because there are more than seventy roads with the word peach tree in it, and it has the largest Hindu temple in the world outside India. I thank you.'

'I concur,' I said, as Mr Know All received a thunderous burst of applause.

'How can I get my old lady away from her fancy man?' shouted another man.

'I don't do personal problems, but maybe you could start by taking a shower,' he said, and more laughter ensued.

'Name the Arsenal Invincibles,' Piers Morgan asked again.

'I thought I'd already explained,' he said, struggling to keep his cool.

And then he really took flight, by not only naming the six wives of Henry VIII but all the winners of Strictly Come Dancing since the show began in 2004, starting with Natasha Kaplinsky. Then, just when you thought he might want to move on, Piers Morgan was back to ask the same football question once more.

'Before I answer anything else, can I ask you a question in return, Mr Morgan?' Mr Know All replied.

'Be my guest.'

'What is proctalgia?' he asked.

'I have no idea,' replied Piers.

'It's the medical term for a pain in the arse.' That brought the house down.

And if that wasn't great enough, the show wound up with a superlative medley of hits from Sir Tom Jones, who got us all rocking in the aisles, even Pearl, and the guy seated next to her took her by the arm and gave her a darn fine jive, which was just what she needed to get into the swing of things.

But it became more than a quick dance together, as he obviously wanted to get to know Pearl better, and while I admired her pulling power – go girl! – I was worried that she would be led astray, being untutored in the ways of men, even if she used to be one. Well his mama would certainly never have taught him, never realizing how he would turn out, while all his father's little talks about how to treat a girl had clearly fallen on deaf ears. Still, Stan the Man was now all woman – well, very nearly – and we'd all just have to get our heads around it, like this guy who'd whisked her away, with Pearl clinging on to his arm, thrilled to be escorted by him – the little strumpet! So much for me having a companion for the evening.

When we got back into the green room I made sure to keep an eagle eye on my friend Pearl and what she might get up to. It almost felt like the responsibility of motherhood. And while I got lumbered with a rather grumpy Piers Morgan, who was still complaining about being the butt of Mr Know All's big joke, I could see Pearl working the room, circulating faster than blood. She was no longer attached to the dancing guy, having upgraded to Sir Tom Jones no less, and he flirted with her mercilessly while she laughed at all his jokes and admired his manly charms as if she'd been born to it.

Then, before you could say 'who's that loose woman?,' Pearl was back by my side, having partaken of a touch too much hospitality, and I saw Piers Morgan's eyes light up.

'So, who's this little filly?' he asked. She giggled right back at him, getting him all frisky, which he'd never managed while in my company.

'Oh, you are a naughty man Piers, winding up Mr Know All like that,' she mock-reprimanded him. 'I've got a good mind to give your botty a big smack.'

OMG! She must have been sozzled, but did Piers care?

'If you must,' he replied to my horror. 'Let's go and find somewhere where you can discipline me as you see fit.'

A man of his age ought to have known better, taking advantage of a tipsy girl like Pearl.

'Please excuse us,' I said to the now-animated TV host as I dragged Pearl kicking and screaming to the ladies' rest room, where I would hopefully sober her up.

'Are you having a good time, Miss Pearl?' I enquired of her.

'I most certainly am,' she replied. 'And it's true what they say about Tom Jones. He said he'd be delighted if I threw my knickers at him, in his dressing room in about half an hour's time.'

'I'm pleased for you, but perhaps a touch more decorum. You don't want to get a name for yourself, do you Pearl?'

'Huh! You can talk. After all, you're my role model and like you, I'm only wanting to be sociable.'

What could I say? 'Do as I say, not as I do,' I tried explaining to her.

'I'm ready to leave anyway,' Pearl said. 'Would you be OK if I disappeared?'

'Sure, of course Pearl. You want to get back home – that's entirely understandable. It can't have been easy for you, your first night out as a woman. Best to get some rest.'

She looked at me if I'd just landed from a distant galaxy. I had obviously got the wrong end of the lollipop.

'The night is young, girlfriend,' she said.

Where did she learn to speak like this?

'That guy I was dancing with – he's a DJ specializing in 1980s discos. He just happens to be gigging in Brixton tonight, and he's asked if I'd like to come up and see his deck sometime.'

Oh Lordy, that's only one letter away from the word dick. The phrase 'lamb to the slaughter' came to mind.

'Pearl honey, are you sure that's wise?' I said, sounding like my mom.

'You're obsessed, Caro,' she said. 'Honestly, it's not what you think.'

'It never is.'

'All it is, he's going to let me have a play on his deck – that's his equipment which plays the tunes. It could be the start of a whole new career for me – Pearl The Girl plays the hits of the eighties, nineties and noughties.'

Well a girl's got to have a career.

'The gig doesn't wind up to six am, and he says I can crash out at his place.'

'You bet your sweet bippy he does. Let me speak to this beau of yours – what's his name?'

'Dave,' she replied.

'How original. Go get him,' I ordered her, like a bossy mom.

When they both returned I gave him a piece of my

mind about how he needn't think he could take advantage of my young friend Pearl, and if he did, he would have me to answer to. He looked suitably chastened. So that's what was going on in his mind.

'And you're OK about being on your own tonight?' she said.

Is there anything worse than being patronized by someone who knows so much less than you?

'Of course, I'm OK. You don't think I ever really believed any of that conspiracy crap, do you?'

'It hasn't rained for ages,' she said, testing my resolve.

'Shut up Pearl, go have fun playing with your decks,' I instructed her. Decks indeed – but then why was I being so protective? It's not like she was going to get pregnant.

So, there I was, a supposed man magnet, nursing my glass of pinot all on my own, when I became conscious of a tall, dark, unshaven gentleman looking at me from a distance. He wasn't really my type, a little too scruffy for my taste. Then veteran DJ Tony Blackburn stepped up to congratulate me on my radio show. It got even better when an eye-catchingly statuesque middle-aged lady I instantly recognized as Valerie Leon from the Carry On films came up to me. I'm such a big Carry On fan.

'Oh darling, I just loved the way you put down that horrible comedian,' she said. 'Nothing like a good dick joke to cut a man down to size - is there, Tony?' He began to smile and blush.

I couldn't believe that an icon like Valerie Leon was congratulating lil' ol' me.

'Oh, I am not worthy. I just loved you in all those Carry On films, and you still look great,' I just had to tell her.

'Too kind,' she said. 'And it's so lovely to get compliments for my work from a young woman, although these days I struggle to remember too much about it. There again, sometimes it only seems like yesterday when we were all down there at Pinewood. Do you know what, we used to get attacked for being sexist, but now I'm even referred to as a feminist icon.'

'Definitely a feminist icon for me. In the Carry On movies, the girls were always the ones calling the shots while the guys – if you can call them that – were always doing what you darn well told them to do.'

'Now you mention it,' she replied with a smile.

'And it was kind of inspiring for the likes of me how you proved that a tall girl can be sexy too, especially in that scene in Carry On Girls when you go from being the prim and proper shy girlfriend to the upfront glamour girl in the bathing beauty contest, like some saucy Cinderella.'

'You really do know your Carry Ons, although personally I would have loved to be in the cat fight with lovely Babs and the divine Dawn Breaks. That's the part most people seem to remember from the movie.'

'That must have been so much fun,' I agreed. 'You would have had them both for breakfast.'

'Well there wasn't much in the way of male totty on

the set, darling. All Bernie, my so-called boyfriend in the film, really cared about was being dressed up by Babs as a beauty queen in his wig and swimsuit, bless him. Thank heavens for Sid – he was the only who could get it up.' She whispered into my ear. 'Less acting required when doing a scene with Sid, if you know what I mean, darling.' We both rolled around giggling while Tony looked on, slightly bewildered.

Then, always in demand, she was called away to another group of well-wishers. I could only hope I would look that good and have such a smart sense of humor when I got to her age.

But after the sheer joy of Valerie, I went and got myself burdened with the most miserable-looking man in the room, the tall, unshaven guy I mentioned earlier. I do confess, I could have done without him hanging around. It was guaranteed to drag a girl down from the high of having a new famous friend to the reality of chatting to a complete no-hoper. See how shallow I had become since becoming addicted to my new celebrity lifestyle? The least I could do was to flash an encouraging smile for him to come and join me, even if only for a short time, after which I would get back to being vain again.

'We need to talk,' he said, obviously not one for beating around the bush.

'If you say so,' I replied, trying to keep everything light and above board.

'Your life is in danger unless you get out of London as soon as possible.'

'Well, I know house prices are a bit on the high side, but I don't think that constitutes a risk to my life.'

'They want me dead too – and not without reason. I am a lifelong opponent of the Project, and they are almost certainly waiting for us outside with some kind of toxin or gas.'

'Perhaps that Piers Morgan could be one of them too.'

'I don't get the impression you're taking any of this seriously. May I introduce myself. My name is Vlad.'

'Caroline Kennedy. Sorry if you think I'm being rude, sweetheart, but I've heard it all before on Into The Night. Not that I believe everything the Government tells us, nor any other government for that matter. Nor do I deny the existence of some deranged people in the world who want to wreak havoc on us all by working together through religious, political or national affiliations.'

'I don't disagree with anything you've said so far,' he said encouragingly.

'I might look like a bimbo, but I don't think like one – well, not most of the time.' I smiled.

'People always seem surprised to get brains and beauty in the same package, as if nobody could be that fortunate,' he said.

Suddenly I was kind of glad this guy had hooked up with me – such a perceptive and thoughtful individual. Who needs more C list celebs?

'But there are so many insane ideas doing the rounds these days. And as for all that hateful stuff about a Jewish conspiracy – haven't their people suffered enough already? It makes me want to hurl,' I said.

'My thoughts entirely,' he said. 'How refreshing for somebody like you to take on those keyboard warriors, sitting at their PCs in their underpants. But I'm very far from one of those, Miss Kennedy, because I have the evidence right here in my pocket that a hugely powerful cabal of what are often referred to as populist world leaders has paid trillions for a groundbreaking scientific secret that could fatally compromise the future of our world.'

Suddenly this was doing my head in, but not in a bad way, as he obviously knew what he was talking about. And who was I to argue with him?

'Is this to do with the weather?' I asked him. 'It's true that it hasn't rained for weeks, and I should know, for I'm a weather girl of some disrepute. Or is it to do with too many female hormones in the sea? I have a vested interest in this one – they're turning our menfolk all sissy, makin' them want to dress up in ladies' clothing instead of reproducing the species and makin' out with hot girls like me.'

'I can see why that last one would give you concern, although I'm not sure who could benefit from it. But controlling the weather has been the dream of man since time immemorial,' he explained.

'So? I'm still no wiser,' I said, somewhat dumbfounded.

'It's probably best I say no more, except that the Project, mistakenly I now believe, think you already know too much and want you dead.'

I looked on enviously at all those shiny, happy people surrounding us gossiping away about who was doing what with whoever, while I was stuck with a guy who only wanted to talk scarily about how my life was under threat.

'Then I'd better go to the cops right away, even though Inspector Flowers assured me I had nothing to worry about.'

'I really don't see the point, Miss Kennedy. They'd only lock you up for wasting police time. It's you and me against the Project, I'm afraid.'

'Well nobody's going to harm me in my own home, and if you want to come and join me, sure, let's take them on together,' I said, and he readily agreed. You can take the girl out of the Atlanta Volunteer Corps, but you sure can't take the Atlanta Volunteer Corps out of the girl.

All the way home in the cab Vlad was looking uneasily behind us to see who might be following. Occasionally he asked the driver to turn left or swing right at short notice. We were taking the most bizarre route possible, obviously to put any potential pursuer off the scent.

When we got back to my place, Vlad stumbled as he got out the taxi. He'd been distracted by an insect biting him on the face, one of the down sides of living by the

Heath in summer. He still had the sense to survey the surrounding terrain for signs of potential assassins, but he soon gave the all clear and gestured for me to go inside. We locked the doors securely behind us, so not even Pearl with her own set of keys could enter.

Once inside, Vlad advised that we should go upstairs to get a clear view of anything that might be happening outside, and sure enough, there under the lamp post stood two burly middle-aged men in long overcoats and Homburg hats.

'Out there – look! – can you see them? They'll be agents from the Project,' he explained.

'Shall I call my tame policeman?' I suggested.

'Not a good idea. They'll be monitoring our calls, and contacting the police would be their cue to come in and slaughter us.'

I was wondering what in the Lord's name I"d gotten myself into. We shut the drapes on them, and no sooner had we done so than the landline started ringing.

'Don't pick up,' Vlad instructed me. 'It'll be them trying to unsettle us. Just let it ring.'

'But it might be my friend Pearl, she's out on the town for the first time with a gentleman friend tonight. She's very naïve and the Lord only knows what scrapes she might have got herself into,' I explained as the phone continued to ring incessantly.

'She could contact you on your cell phone if she's got herself into a pickle,' he rightly advised.

I thought the best place for me might be in the

kitchen for a short while, popping some pizza into the microwave for Vlad, which he devoured like a man who hadn't eaten since sun up. And then over coffee he gave me some stuff for safe keeping, including a map of the Derbyshire Peak District, a USB stick which he said contained an algorithm for a scientific breakthrough of some description, and a bottle of pills, which he refused to elaborate on further, while all the time the radio was playing Freddie Mercury singing *Who Wants To Live Forever*, one of my favourite ever songs.

'The less I tell you, the better it will be if you get caught,' he said. 'If anything happens to me, you must take these things to an address in Derbyshire, which I will give you in the morning. But first I must sleep – it's been a long day.' He looked as shattered as he sounded.

I asked him if he would object sleeping head to toe – this really was becoming something of a habit. Once again I didn't fancy sleeping alone, not with those goons outside ready to strike. And he was only too happy to oblige. The last thing he told me before we climbed into our respective ends was to beware of a man with a scar under his right eye. 'He cannot be trusted,' said Vlad.

Considering the almighty mess we seemed to have found ourselves in, I slept remarkably soundly, and when I woke Vlad still appeared to be deep in the land of nod. I went downstairs to make a cup of tea for him, but when I returned to deliver him the drink and gave him a nudge, there was no response. Perhaps he would have preferred coffee?

'Vlad, wake up,' I said. I said it again, louder. Then I shook him, but he didn't stir. That was when I began to wonder if something dreadful had befallen him in his sleep. My mind went back to that insect bite. Perhaps it hadn't been an insect bite at all. Perhaps it was a poisoned dart... well, you do read of such things, don't you?

I felt for his pulse, and there was absolutely nothing there.

Just then the phone in the spare room rang. I answered it.

'Is he dead yet?' a voice with a thick East European accent enquired.

'Yes, I believe he is,' I honestly replied.

'Good. Unless you hand over the algorithm, you'll be next.'

'Go to hell!' I shouted back at him and slammed the phone down.

Although I don't frighten easy, I finally realised that it was time to get the hell out of there and go some place safe. Just then I heard the milkman singing outside on the front doorstep, and had one of my occasional moments of clarity – I would use him to help me escape. I think I'd seen something similar in an old black and white movie, but this was gonna be my version. Playing the damsel in distress card, I ran down and asked him in.

'I seem to be in the most dreadful predicament. What's a girl supposed to do?' I pleaded with him.

'How can I help?' he replied.

'There are two private investigators outside who've been trailing me. My husband has hired them because he thinks I've been having an affair, which I have, because he's cold and cruel towards me. Not like you, I'm sure – a girl can tell if a man knows how to treat a woman, and you look like a man of the world who understands that a woman has needs too.'

'I so do,' he said, staring at me with big round eyes. He had taken the bait. Most men are hard wired to be chivalrous.

'So here's the thing, could I could borrow your uniform and milk cart so I can get out of here without them recognising me? Otherwise my husband will have me killed. He has friends in very high places.'

'Nobody gets killed on my round!' said the milkman heroically. He agreed to go upstairs to change into some of Stan's old clothes while I put on his white pants and jacket. I grabbed a large pair of scissors from the kitchen to complete the look by cutting off my hair, much to the horror of the milkman. I was sure going to miss those long lustrous blonde locks which got me noticed wherever I went. But perhaps it would be a relief not to get stared at for a while. I stuffed the shorn hair into my overnight bag along with a couple of wigs for additional disguise, should I need it, plus, most important of all, my Rampant Rabbit vibrator. Not the same as the real thing, of course – it's better. Who says you can't improve on nature? And you don't have to wash and iron its underpants either.

'Ready when you are, milkman,' I said to him. 'Not the first time you've heard that from one of your lady customers, eh?'

'You nip out the back door, while I go out the front and take your cart and park it around the corner in Antrobus Road,' I ordered, handing him my overnight bag.

'Will do, ma'am' he replied, as a man in uniform should.

So I stepped out in his outfit while he left by the back door. It all went according to plan – until I climbed on the cart and drove it backwards into a wall with a great crashing and clanking of bottles. I had put it into reverse.

'Ooops!' I said in a decidedly female voice, placing my hand over my mouth like a girl. Hellfire, that wouldn't do. I had to try and rescue the situation before the private dicks got suspicious. 'Farkin' 'ell,' I roared in a low-pitched gravelly Cockney-style voice. It seemed to be convincing enough to stand down the heavies who'd been monitoring our house all night, while murdering Vlad in the process. Whistling a happy tune, I powered that cart right out of there.

Round the back, I hooked up with the real milkman at our pre-arranged pick-up point. He had my overnight bag in his hand.

'You made it,' he said.

'You too. You're my hero,' I said, kissing him on both

cheeks, before slipping away into a nearby wood where I disrobed from my milkman's gear and put on one of Stan's suits. I disguised my curves as best as I could to create the illusion that I was of the male persuasion.

'What do you reckon?' I asked the milkman upon my return.

'Too much like a man for my taste,' he observed. 'I much preferred you as a girl.' Just what I wanted to hear.

"Now please don't believe everything you're gonna read in the papers and see on TV about me,' I implored him. 'You've done nothing wrong by helping me, and I promise you almost all of it will be fake.'

'You can trust in me,' he said sweetly. 'My name's Bob, by the way.'

'Have you ever been kissed by a boy, Bob?'

'I can't say I have.'

'Well you have now,' I said and kissed him full on the lips as his reward. Hopefully I had bought his silence for a short while after the police got hold of him.

'Then I waved him goodbye and headed for the Underground. I went straight to Euston Station, where I called Pearl to let her know what the hell had been going down.

'What time is it?' she asked, as if I'd just woken her up.

'It's still quite early but I need you here, Miss Pearl,' I explained.

'But I've been up all night gigging with Dave.'

'I never doubted it,' I said. I could hear Dave's voice saying, 'why don't you get back into bed?'The little minx. What is it with young women these days, giving out on their first dates?

'I wouldn't ask you to come all the way over to Euston unless it was important, Pearl. Meet me at the top of the escalator, and whatever you do, don't go back home first,' I warned her in the gravest of tones.

'Caro, you're starting to frighten me now. OK, I'll be there just as soon as I can,' she promised.

While I waited for her to arrive, I passed the time doing a little window shopping, and I couldn't help but notice that nobody was window-shopping me anymore. Suddenly, I was no longer turning heads. I'd become a guy, the kind nobody bothers to look at twice. It felt kind of liberating too to be freed from the chains of always being on show, although I wasn't sure how long I would want it to last. A couple of appreciative looks from girls would have been nice though.

I popped into a branch of Victoria's Secret, where I received one or two questioning looks – didn't these people realize I modelled for them on TV? Obviously not. And why should they, looking the way I did? This was exactly what I wanted if I was to travel unrecognized once I headed north.

When Pearl finally emerged from the Underground, still looking defiantly resplendent on her first walk of shame, she couldn't believe her eyes when she got sight of me. In fact, she didn't even recognize me at first and walked right past as if I didn't exist. The stiletto was now most certainly on the other foot.

'Pearl!' I shouted after her. 'It's me, Caro!'

'Oh my god! Why are you dressed as Stan? Is there something you want to tell me?'

'It's only a temporary arrangement,' I assured her, 'until I get back to Wolverhampton, where I'm going to hook up with Larry.'

'Are you sure he's going to appreciate the new look, with you dressed as me?'

'No chance. I have to tell you Pearl, this is worse than complicated. Let me explain.'

A few minutes later we were in the American Diner, where we ordered pancakes and crispy bacon, washed down by filter coffee.

'There's no simple way of saying this, Pearl,' I said, fiddling with the lapel of my man's jacket. 'I took a guy home last night and he finished up dead.' I was still trying to make sense of it myself.

'What am I supposed to say?'

'You could try screaming, that would be a traditionally feminine thing to do. Except us girls have got so much cooler now.'

'Too right,' she said.

I then recounted how I'd met Vlad after talking to my new best friend, Valerie Leon, and the way it progressed, with us finishing up head to toe in my bed, but not before he'd scared me witless with talk of something called The Project, and how they wanted to kill me, while two murderous gangsters lurked outside the house.

'Now that's truly scary,' she replied.

'And he gave me this package to deliver, but no address, while Freddie Mercury sang 'Who Wants To Live Forever' on the radio.

'Great tune.'

'I'll never forget it. Then the next thing I know Vlad's as dead as a hog at throat-slittin' time. More bacon, Pearl? I don't think he died of natural causes – we didn't have sex or anything like that. I suspect he might have been murdered, but not by me, obviously.'

'You poor thing,' she said.

'Of course, the cops are never going to believe any of this – not even Inspector Flowers. I've got maniacs out there wanting to kill me, so I need to disappear, Pearl. I've got to get the hell out of London while I can.'

'Of course – whatever it takes. We'll be just like Thelma and Louise, the two of us against the world.'

'I don't think so. They both finished up dead, whereas there's only going to be one of me, and I'm most definitely plannin' on stayin' alive. You'd be more help to me hanging out in London, hun, although I really do appreciate the offer.' Pearl looked crestfallen.

'You don't think losing all your lovely hair has affected your head?' she said.

'Plus, I'm going back to Larry.'

'You've just answered my question.'

'It's not as crazy as it sounds.'

'Does he know yet?'

'Not exactly.'

'How exactly not exactly?'

'OK, not at all.'

'Sounds like a plan, Caro – not!'

'So, what I need from you, Pearl, is for you to pretend to go back to the house as if you knew absolutely nothing, then when you see Vlad lying there, dead in my bed, go running out into the street and shout...'

'Murder most foul?'

'Maybe something just a little less Agatha Christie, like, oh my gahd, there's a stiff in Caro's bed?'

'No change there then.'

'Nobody likes a smartass, Pearl. Just say it however you want to phrase it. And don't tell the cops about us meeting here – not even Inspector Flowers. Just let stuff unfold naturally, until I can shake off these guys who want to kill me and prove my innocence.'

'You make it all sound so simple, Caro. The way Stephen Hawking's A Brief History Of Time is simple.'

'Sorting me out with Larry is going to take a little longer,' I finally admitted. Then I gave her a big hug goodbye, told her to carry on being herself and to contact Carla, so that she could take my place as stand-in on my show, not as Stan the Man but Pearl the Girl.

'You think she'd buy that?'

'I'm damn sure she will, honey,' I replied. Then I left, heading off to a place just off the North Circular Road where all the truck drivers hung out, to see if I could get a ride north.

Truly, I was on my way.

PART TWO

INTO THE FIGHT

'Give a girl the right shoes and she can conquer the world'

Marilyn Monroe

CHAPTER EIGHT

Having reached the café where all the truckers hung out, I hesitated for a moment, not too sure if my disguise would be convincing enough to fool those macho drivers. I seemed to have passed the gender test riding up on the subway, as I'd gone pretty much unnoticed by the commuters. But then you could be dressed as Ronald McDonald in high heels on the London Underground and you would barely get a second glance.

I still felt there was something lacking about my disguise, a certain stick of dynamite to give me the swagger of a real alpha guy.

Not far from the Truckers' Café there was a greengrocer's stall. 'I'll take one of your biggest courgettes, mate,' I asked the guy. He duly handed one over, then I skedaddled around the corner, where I placed it strategically down my pants. I had thought of deploying a couple of onions too, but that could have been a vegetable (or two) too far. Now I really felt the part – and what a part!

Then, just as I was about to join my fellow guys inside the café for a spot of willy wanging, or whatever it is they do, I noticed out of the corner of my eye a pretty young woman who was also hesitating on whether to go in. Who could blame her?

'They won't bite, love – not unless you want them to!' I said, trying to lighten her load with an unreconstructed sexist joke. It's called getting into character.

'Are you going in there?' she asked.

'You'd be very welcome to join me, if it helps.'

'That would be really kind of you,' she said.

'Are you a trucker too?' she asked, her eyes darting down to my pants, taking aim at my courgette.

'No, but I could introduce you to one, if you're looking for a ride some place,' I politely offered.

The girl was gushing in her thanks. She had clearly seen something in me that she could relate to, and was only too grateful to have somebody to accompany her into this stridently masculine place where you could sniff the testosterone in the air.

No sooner had we entered than it was as if we had switched off their conversations. My presence headed off all the usual sexist comments and catcalls which would have erupted had a man not been with her.

'Two teas love,' I said to the waitress behind the counter, having now perfected my male voice. She gave me a smile that would have been enough to make my courgette quiver, had it been hooked up to the rest of me.

'So, where are you going?' I asked my companion upon returning to the table carrying teas.

She said she was travelling to Solihull – same direction as me – and her name was Wanda.

'And I'm Carl. I'm going a little further north, to Wolverhampton. We could ride together if you like?'

'Oh, that would be *soooo* lovely,' she said, sounding highly relieved. 'I don't know why but I feel there's something about you I can trust, as if you're on my wavelength.'

'Weird,' I observed back in a monosyllabic male way.

'Some of these drivers think you owe it to have sex with them – as if my sparkling conversation wasn't payment enough for a free ride.'

I recognized her slightly self-deprecating female sense of humor, not unlike mine – but now I was no-nonsense Carl, maybe Carla's long-lost half-brother.

'Don't worry, you'll be safe with me love, unless you don't want to be,' I said. 'Hopefully they'll think we're an item and leave you alone.'

She blushed. 'Do you know what?' she said, 'I don't mind if they do think we're a couple if it helps get them off my back. Maybe we could hold hands in the cab together?'

The little minx – as if dealing with Pearl wasn't testing enough.

'I really don't mind if you want to,' she added.

'Result!' I was even beginning to think like a guy.

But first we had to beg a free ride, not easy when it's boy and girl together. When it comes to hitching a ride, a guy's about as welcome as a one-legged man at an arse kicking contest. It didn't look promising at first, until I heard a familiar voice, as if I was back on the radio.

'Does any bugger know where you can munch a half-decent piece of pickled beetroot round here?' this crazy trucker said. I'm not sure if he was really listening, which was so typical of Olaf. Yes, Olaf the Polish truck driver, who regularly appeared on my show. What were the chances, him turning up like that? It felt like greeting an old friend, although I didn't dare show it for fear of giving away my real identity. I bribed him with tea and hot buttered toast, which seemed to soften him enough to let me come on board for the journey north.

'The girl sits next to me though,' he demanded.

'You're so much better than that, Olaf. The girl goes where she wants,' I insisted. I had nearly given my identity away by being so assertive, but not quite. Wanda asked to sit by the passenger door, which made him a touch grumpy at first, with me next to Olaf instead, poor love. If only he'd known.

I surveyed all those pictures from my gallery of shame of me in various stages of undress, plastered around his cab. You could tell Wanda approved of the seating arrangements by the way she stroked my arm, flicked my hair and rubbed cream into my hands, leaving Olaf to his own devices as we thundered up the M40.

'I love pickling stuff,' he unaccountably said out of nowhere. 'Us Poles are the best in the world at it. You should taste my pickled sausage'. Anything to get the spotlight back on him.

'You don't say,' I said without trying to disguise my disinterest, while Wanda flashed me a knowing smile.

Then I thought of how Carla would have smiled at my lesbian goings on, and maybe Wanda would have been my type, if that's what nature had intended for me. She was a good few inches shorter than me, which made me feel surprisingly protective towards her. And why wouldn't I, with her emerald green eyes and her decidedly kissable lips? Maybe I was gay, but just hadn't met the right lady until now – a confusing thought for a girl to have on her way to look up a guy called Larry, who she still regarded as the love of her life, in Wolverhampton.

While Wanda and I held hands, Olaf made do with his radio, flicking around the dial until he landed upon Capital Talk, which was trailing the night time show with Pearl the Girl. My heart leapt.

'What, no Caro?' said a distraught Olaf.

'Go, Pearl,' I said, genuinely thrilled that Pearl the Girl's radio career was taking flight.

'No way, I'm not having it! Miss Caro's my absolute

favorite,' raged Olaf. 'I phone in plenty, and even when I just listen to show she keep me happy. What am I to do?'

'Well I think she's trashy,' I couldn't resist saying.

'That's so not true,' said Wanda, pointedly letting go of my hand. 'She's a feminist icon, treating men the way men have been treating women for years. Thanks to Miss Caro, we're getting our own back.'

'Oh Lordy, is that how you see her?'

'From what I've read, if she wants a man, she goes and gets him. What's not to like about that, Carl? Or are you too much of a bloke to get it?' She was running her hand up and down my left thigh.

'It's a point of view, I sp'ose,' I said, starting to feel a touch aroused. I know I was on a sex diet, but I was starting to wonder whether Wanda would really count as one of my five a day.

'But Miss Caro's so much more than that,' Olaf declared, God bless him. 'How many times has she been hurt in love? She goes on about it on her show all the time, and she wants to settle down. I'd do anything to help her.'

Just as I'd been elevated to the sainthood by Olaf, along came a news bulletin which threatened to send me right back to hell. It announced that the body of a dissident Russian scientist had been found in the home of Capital Talk's very own Caroline Kennedy, and that she had gone missing.

'Go girl!' said Wanda, which personally I thought

was taking feminism a bit too far. Olaf looked deeply concerned. 'Poor Caro, I'm there for you baby,' he said to nobody in particular, but I took it anyway. Everybody was talking about me – how strange to see yourself as others see you. Now that Vlad's body had been found, those heavies who wanted to kill me would have been alerted to the strong likelihood that I was now on the run, and had probably guessed that I'd already quit London. And they would come looking for me, as would the cops, especially when the next bulletin revealed that I was now wanted on suspicion of murder.

'She's definitely innocent,' said Olaf. 'I am Polish, and I know what these Russians are capable of.'

'They're not all bad, Olaf,' I counselled him. 'It's just the guy in charge and those oligarchs. The Russians love their children too – just ask Sting.'

'But we've seen what happens to their double agents in Salisbury,' said Wanda. 'I don't think poor Caro will get far, do you Carl?'

'Oh, I don't know – I think she'll be just fine,' I replied with undue confidence.

'I'm *sooooo* glad you think so – I just adore a guy who can see stuff from a feminine perpective as well,' said Wanda. She kissed me full on the lips, and I kissed her back without hesitation. Those generous, pouty lips of hers pressing against these generous pouty lips of mine created a bed of female lippy lusciousness of a kind I'd never experienced before. I thought, I could get to like this, if I live long enough to be worthy of a woman's love.

'Hey, no more lovey dovey stuff in my cab, unless it's with me,' Olaf ordered.

Wanda whispered in my ear, 'you've made me moist'.

Me too, I wanted to reply, but instead I owned up to loving somebody else. I didn't want another woman to be misled, the fate of most of our sex.

'I thought so. I just knew you were too good to be true,' she said.

We had reached her designated drop-off point in Solihull, and Olaf brought his truck to a juddering stop.

'It was nothing more than a beautiful moment,' she declared after I'd helped her out of the cab with her luggage. 'But I'm going to find it so hard to forget you.' She pressed her body hard against my courgette, loving it more than any vegetable has a right to be loved.

'I've never been so flattered – what a man! You'd spoil me for any other guy.'

And then Olaf blasted his horn.

'I've never met a guy like you before,' said Wanda.

'And you probably never will again,' I replied as I made my way back to the cab. I blew her kisses while we set off to continue on our way north.

'Love 'em and leave 'em, eh Olaf?' I said. Now there was a man talking.

'Hey, she's crazy for you. What's your secret?' he enquired.

'You've got a sausage, I've got a courgette. Maybe she's a vegetarian?'

'Sometimes I don't understand you crazy English,' he said, cutting up another innocent car driver.

'I'm not English, I'm American.'

'Oh, like Caro.'

'Exactly like Caro. I come from the same city in the deep south.'

'You know her?' said Olaf, getting excited.

'In a manner of speaking. Sometimes I don't seem to know her at all.'

'I don't understand that either.'

'What you said about Miss Caro back there, believing without any shadow of a doubt that she's innocent – it really touched me. I reckon she could trust you not to give her away.'

'One hundred and eleven per cent she could,' he said.

So I decided it was time to open my heart to Olaf. I asked him to stop at the next service station, so I could change back into Caro. I guessed the milkman would have cracked under interrogation by now and revealed that I'd escaped dressed as a young man. I needed to woman up, and what a delight it was to liberate my breasts and let them breathe once more. I will never complain about wearing a bra again. And how wondrous to apply make-up, put on a silk blouse and a knee-length skirt and best of all, high heels. How could guys ever live without these bare necessities? I couldn't put my long hair back, so I dug out a wild, eye-catching red-haired wig. I popped my courgette into my handbag as a keepsake.

I was a woman again, but I couldn't deny enjoying my moments with Wanda. I was surprised by how close we'd become in such a short time, and mentally added making whoopee with a gorgeous girl to my bucket list, although exactly how I was going to square it with the man of my dreams, I hadn't quite worked out. I sashayed back to Olaf's truck in all my blessed womanliness, swaying side to side powered by pure feminine motion and flicking my shock of hair – I'd always fancied being a redhead.

'Oh, my beloved Polskie, you're wearing women's clothes. You must be Transylvanian!' said a shocked-sounding Olaf upon seeing my transformation.

'You sure know how to make a girl feel good about herself, Olaf. I think you mean transvestite, and no, I'm most certainly not.'

'But I saw you kissing that girl, and you had big sausage, which is why she liked you.'

'I already told you, it was a courgette,' I said, pulling it out and handing it to him as a souvenir. 'You might get a coupla bucks for that on eBay if you're lucky, or maybe a little more if you tell folks where it's been.'

Poor Olaf. What had he done to deserve all this confusion I was inflicting on him? It was time to put him out of his misery.

'Hi y'all, and welcome back to my front porch, why not pull up a chair?' I said.

'Oh, my gracious goodness – it's you, isn't it? You're

Miss Caro, but with bright red hair, in my cab, sitting right next to me!'

'Calm down Olaf,' I said. He had begun hyperventilating, and he was starting to lose control of his truck. 'I need you to be strong for me, and help get me out of this dreadful predicament I've got myself into. But first, I need you to keep this friggin' machine on the goddam highway!'

'Yes, I must pull myself together,' he said as cars, coaches and other trucks all swerved to avoid him.

'That's better Olaf – hands on the wheel, eyes on the road ahead.'

'I'm getting there.'

''Good, 'cos I've got these crazy guys chasing me. They want to kill your favorite radio show host, and the cops think I'm a murderin' bitch from hell. Can you see what a fandango of a pickle I'm in?'

'What do you want me to do? I will do anything. I will take you back to Polska in back of my truck. You'd be safe in there, with plenty of sausage and beetroot to eat.'

'That's a real kind thought, Olaf. But first I need you to take me to my ex-boyfriend's boat, which is in a canal just outside Wolverhampton. I'm figurin' on lying low there for a while until the heat dies down.'

I was already talking like a criminal on the run.

'Ex-boyfriend? Not sure about that,' said Olaf. 'Not that bar steward who let you down after proposing marriage to you at your wedding to somebody else? You know, to the one with the sleepy head who stood you up at the altar well knowing that he's not great enough for you, and then this other one, having proposed, goes and dumps you too – the love of your life that you're always going on about on your blessed show.'

'Nicely put, Olaf,' I said. Well, it was complicated.

'Is that wise, Caroline?'

'You can call me Miss Caro.'

'But can you trust him?'

'My secret will be safe with him, Olaf. Larry's a good man who will know what to do to sort this whole darn mess out.'

'Just 'cos he's great in the sack doesn't make him a good man, Caro.'

'He's so much more than that. It's not just about the sex when it comes to Larry. He used to be my rock, you know.'

'But then he let you down, so now you need a new man, or maybe it's time for that nice girl Wanda, but never go back Caro, it's time to move on,' advised Olaf, very much from the heart.

'That sounded like a Miss Caro kind of thing to say.'

'You see how I've been listening over the months and years.'

'You've learnt well, Olaf. There's no way I'm going back to resurrect an old relationship. I simply need to know why he got rid of me, and only then can I move on,' I said. I was struggling to explain the thoughts which swirled around in my head.

'Caro, leave the past in the past, where it belongs – that's also a Miss Caro kind of thing to say, don't you think?'·

'I need to go back to go forward. That's Miss Caro too, 'cos I'm saying it. And don't forget, he's got a boat, which will make a great place to hide from all those crazy guys who want me dead, while the real murderer will be hunted down by Inspector Flowers, who is convinced of my innocence.'

'I don't like your plan, not one single little bit. You should stay with me,' he said, clearly unimpressed.

'That's so sweet of you, Olaf. Watch that freakin' car!' I screamed at him, but he carried on yakking regardless.

'And this boat guy – he's plenty rich?' Olaf enquired, cutting up another motorist in the inside lane.

'Not really – it was the fact that he wasn't obsessed by money, or his career, that drew me to him,' I tried to explain.

'So, he's a fantastic lover.'

'That's strictly between me and him.'

'And your ten million listeners, who you tell everything about Mr. Boat guy.'

'OK, so he always knew how to put a smile on my face, in so many ways.'

'So, he does have big sausage?'

'There's more to a man than just that, Olaf. So what if he does? I'm a sucker for those big strong arms, me. In fact Larry had it all, or that's how it felt at the time.'

'Now we're getting somewhere,' said Detective Inspector Olaf.

'You should have seen him, the first time I ever set eyes on him, stripped to his waist, working in his garden, wearing those tight-fitting jeans, with beads of sweat running down his muscular torso as he scythed his way through the undergrowth, his strong arms sweeping across the jungle of a backyard. I felt so alive and electric watching him'.

'Enough already. You're obsessed.'

'I just sat there in our bedroom, gazing at him for heaven knows how long...'

'You wanted him to fuck you?' said Olaf, putting it so much more coarsely.

'No, I wanted him to ravish me, Olaf, and when he did, it was wondrous.'

'Please stop, I will crash truck,' Olaf begged.

'But it wasn't just the sex – it was finding a man who embodied all those good ol' fashioned masculine values. I could list them – and what's not to like?'

'Everything,' Olaf replied. 'So, you want the fucker back?'

'No way. I just want him to answer a few fundamental questions so I can move on in my life. I already told you that – why aren't you listening to me?'

'Because I'm driving one big fuck off ten-wheeler truck! Not that I mind you talking – it's like listening to your radio show, being broadcast live in my cab, without the bloody adverts, with you sitting right next to me. What could be better than that?'

We carried on yakking like a pair of drunken cowpokes until I began to recognize my old stomping ground, including the Bull and Bush pub, known locally as the Bush, a name which was always guaranteed to make Larry smile, much like my own, which I wore longer in those days. Surely a successful career woman like me should have put all of this behind her by now? I would have had so much to be thankful for if it hadn't been for the guys who were trying to kill me, yet still this part of my life came back to haunt me, like a ghost who wouldn't let go.

'You can drop me anywhere round here,' I advised Olaf.

'I no let you leave,' he said.

'So you're kidnapping me?'

'I only want to keep you safe, until you get your head together. You are all over the place.'

He had a point – wise Olaf – although I couldn't see it at the time.

'At least I give you my number if you get into fuck big trouble,' he said. I stored it in my new temporary pay as you go phone, bought because it wouldn't leave a trail. 'I'll be there for you Caro, and whenever I'm in UK, I'll come running – or even when I'm in Polska, or some other crazy place, I'll do my bloody best.'

Forget the right shoes. With friends like Olaf, how

could I fail to conquer the world? The least he deserved was a great big smacker on the lips.

'You taste of pickles, Olaf,' I said.

'And you taste of beautiful mountains and freshwater streams and sunshine on a sandy beach.'

'Don't let's get carried away.'

'Take care, Caro – I'll be there for you,' he proclaimed, as he helped me to climb out of the cab. I knew the chances were that I'd never see him again. Words not deeds are what most men are about, not putting their money where their mouth is, which is usually right up their raggedy backsides.

Still, I left him with a heavy heart, for I was on my own now. With my overnight bag in hand and my high heels tip-tapping on the cobbled streets, I made my way down the narrow alleys, or ginnels, as they call them around these parts, until I reached the Wolverhampton Canal, where Larry's boat used to be moored. Of course, there was no guarantee it would still be there after all this time – he could have sold it, and taken up white water rafting instead, or he could have embarked on a month-long cruise with his lovely wife and kids. Forgive me for sounding bitter, it's not a good look, I know. So I was mightily relieved to see it moored in its proper and rightful place, just outside Aldersley Junction, if you ever wanna take a look, with the boat's name, *Carpe Diem*, still inscribed on the hull. And seize the day was exactly what we'd both done all those years ago, when he would take me on those romantic voyages on what I used to call our very own love boat.

With Stan safely out of the way on dry land, worried that he might get seasick on the Grand Union Canal, where the only significant motion we were ever likely to encounter would be Larry and me doing it, rocking that boat like it was a-tossin' and a-turnin' in a force ten gale. Some memories never fade, do they? Even after so long I still recall them vividly – cue more fanny flutters. While I still had the key to his boat, it seemed like I never really had the key to his heart, judging by the way he got up and left me. Just that thought alone was enough to trigger a burst of full-on sobbing.

Just then a middle-aged man came sauntering along the bank. Perhaps he thought I was simply suffering from a bout of seasonal hay fever.

'Nice weather for the time of the year,' he said.

'Still no rain, though,' I replied.

'Yes, it's starting to affect levels in the canal, and if it doesn't come soon we could be talking about restricting access to the public,' he said, mansplaining me.

'What a bummer. And they say dumping female hormones into the sea is having an effect on the virility of men,' I womansplained him back.

'You don't say.'

'And would you by any chance know if Larry Arthur is about?' I asked him.

'Who would want to know?'

'You could say I'm a big fan of his. I read all of his articles in Canal Monthly, and I would love to meet up with him, so he can teach me everything he knows.'

'He has quite a few young ladies wanting to come on board, wanting to get their hands on his tiller, yet there never seem to be any male students – I wonder why that could be?' said the extremely annoying man.

'It looks like those female hormones haven't got to Larry yet, which is just as well... er... for his wife.'

'Isn't it just.'

'Nothing in this world appears to be what it's s'posed to be,' I said, which was probably the most meaningless thing I'd ever said in my whole life.

'And you can't be too careful with this epidemic of boat thefts and their belongings. There's no knowing where they might strike next. Now I know you're just another one of Larry's girls I'll leave you in peace, but he won't be back until next Wednesday because he's away in Menorca with his wife and kids. He has a family, did you know?'

'Don't I just,' I replied. 'So, he's back with them for the moment, is he?'

'Solid as a rock, so don't go wasting your time love. He learnt his lesson when he went off with that American whore.'

'What a floozy,' I said, floozy being so much more endearing than whore.

'Aye, she was the one, but now he's back with his

missus for good, and he's asked me to keep an eye on all his possessions. That's why I was checking up on you and his boat.'

'Most civil minded of you,' I said.

'If you'd like to have a peek inside my cruiser while you're at it, then be my guest,' he said. 'It's moored just around the corner.' He had gone all red in the face.

'Most kind, but I'm the kinda girl who only has eyes for Larry's boat.' That was enough to put an end to his interfering ways.

And no sooner had he gone on his way than I walked all the way around the next bend to where *Carpe Diem* was moored. I used my key to unlock the boat, climbing backwards down the rickety steps on which Larry had once taken me. He couldn't even wait for me to climb aboard, romantic old fool that he was. The first thing that hit me was that long-lost aroma of Larry, all musky and manly and masterful – what a shock to my system to breathe in his scent again. Smells are always so much more evocative than pictures. Forget Facebook, it's high time one of those Harvard geeks invented Aromabook. Who wouldn't want to log on for a whiff of their loved one, or their favorite fantasy man or woman, night or day? And just in case you're considering it, I'm patenting that idea.

As I surveyed the cabin, all those magical memories of our cruises came wafting back. I remembered our epic love-making sessions before I returned home to Stan, and how I'd forsaken him once again to join Larry on the other side of the bedroom wall while he lay asleep. I was insatiable for him.

In truth, I don't think I'd ever felt as alive as in those special months, but when I recalled the interfering man's reference to me being just another of Larry's girls, my heart sank at the thought of it. In spite of what he'd claimed, still I refused to doubt Larry. Anyway, at least *Carpe Diem* would provide a place for me to hide away and keep my head down for as long as possible, at least until Larry returned.

If he was continuing to use this as his love boat, then he wasn't keeping it very well stocked, for if music be the food of love, there wasn't too much left to play on. I risked giving myself away by venturing down to the local supermarket – I would at least have to stay out of sight until darkness fell.

I switched on the TV only to see myself in all my infamy on every news channel, the 'Killer in High Heels,' as the BBC gleefully put it. Mercifully my photofit, no doubt created from the milkman's description of me, looked like a young man and was nowhere near how I now appeared now that I was back to my old voluptous self, not to mention a bright red wig as my crowning glory.

I couldn't see them tracking me down for a good while yet, which is why I refused to panic when somebody started knocking on the cabin door. I though it was the interfering man again, but then I heard a shout of 'Open the bloody hell up, Miss Caro, it's only me!'

Never have I been so glad to hear the voice of a Polish trucker. I opened the door, and there was Olaf with a two bagloads of supplies to keep me going until Larry returned. 'Oh, you little beauty!' I said, kissing him on both cheeks.

'No, you're the beauty,' he said. 'You have the best bod in Europe, and I should know, driving backwards and forwards all over the bleeding place. And your smile is bright enough to light up an entire continent. I've got some English crap, plus some brilliant Polskie stuff for you to eat and drink, including Polskie bread, beetroot and pickles, to be washed down with vodka.'

'I don't know how to thank you,' I said to him.

'I've got one or two ideas,' he said with a wicked smile.

That apart, how could I go wrong with Olaf, so loyal and true? And I was glad of his company too, as we played a game of the Warsaw version of Monopoly, which I won, somewhat too triumphantly for his liking. I could tell he was trying to distract me from the mess I was in, at least until he produced a bundle of English newspapers with an array of lurid headlines, all of which related to little 'ol me. Most of them went with the aforementioned killer in high heels, apart from The Sun, which chose 'Death In A Double D Cup,' as if my boobs were somehow responsible for Vlad's demise.

'They think you did it, but they're wrong,' said Olaf.

Plus, there's some great pictures of you in bikinis and kinky lingerie on pages 6, 7 and 8.'

'Haven't you got some washing machines to deliver?' I reminded him.

'I go to fucking Leeds first before I bugger off back to Polska, but I hate to leave you alone, don't I?'

'Please don't worry about me. Larry will be back soon.'

'That's what's worrying me,' he replied, which I could have done without – and he hadn't even met the much-maligned guy.

I guess his hostility to Larry helped make my parting from Olaf easier to handle, although the next few days were about as boring as a hoedown when the moonshine runs dry. And to make matters worse, I'd become bloated by a relentless diet of pickled food and premium-strength vodka. I would have to get my act together and cleanse my body in time for Larry's return. I didn't want him to think I'd somehow let myself go just because I'd been outed as a murdering maniac.

So, in between downing countless glasses of cool fresh water, I endured hearing about my latest ghastly deeds on the news channels. You should have heard how the clips from my radio show sounded once they'd been edited and taken out of context, then cut together with scenes of me in various stages of undress – not a good look for a serious journalist. Somehow, the sexier they made me look, the more guilty it made me seem, as if I should be punished for having the bare-faced temerity to look hot, regardless of whether I'd done anything wrong or not. 'Lock the bitch up!,' I could hear them shouting at their television screens the length and breadth of the country.

'We only have one suspect at this stage of the enquiry,' said the police spokesman. Yep, lil 'ol me was more guilty than a fox caught leaving the hen house with a mouthful of rooster.

Obviously, it couldn't have been Inspector Flowers delivering the bad news – he'd probably already have been sidelined in the enquiry by his superiors for arguing my case. Then came interviews with Carla and Pearl, both protesting my innocence – the Lord bless those two ladies for praising me to the heavens like I was a cross between Mother Theresa and Bette Midler. Carla lauded me for my skills as a fine radio presenter on Into The Night, while Pearl raved about how I'd supported her in her journey from boyfriend to best girlfriend. 'Doesn't mean she didn't do it though,' I could hear the viewers saying, despite all that.

I'd sure done the right thing by lying low in Larry's boat. I only emerged from my metal bunker after sundown to venture forth for a short walk along the towpath, exchanging the odd pleasantry with folks walking their dogs. Then I would batten down the hatches again, spurred on by reminding myself that there were only a couple more days to wait until Larry returned from his family holiday, when he would inevitably pay a visit to his beloved boat.

I would down a couple more of Olaf's cut-price vodkas, reduced in price but not strength, due to the local Polish shop's Special Brexit closing-down sale, and tuck myself into the very same bed where Larry and I had once made out on our love trysts. If only you could flick on a dream like choosing a box set – Larry and Miss Caro make whoopee on their love boat, instead of having to endure pickled Polish beetroot and Olaf singing Elvis.

Suddenly I snapped out of my dream. I had felt a movement on the boat. Then I distinctly felt *Carpe Diem* rocking from side to side, and heard the sound of the boat's engine kicking in. The annoying guy on the towpath had been yakking on about the theft of boats on the canal. Was Larry's boat about to be stolen in a canalside heist, or had those heavy people who wanted me dead tracked me down and were piloting the boat towards a more private location where they could slit my throat and throw me over the side to feed the fishes? Larry wouldn't be back for another two days.

OK, so I was on my own, but I hadn't been a recruit of the Atlanta Defense Force for nothing. Well, it was mostly to meet hot boys bearing arms – not that I'd ever expected to be given special after-hours lessons by the dashing grown-up captain, who ever so kindly took me under his wing and showed me how to operate advanced weaponry. I soon got the hang of it, and he gave me a glowing report. Maybe that's where my obsession for older men first started.

So, what would the good Captain have done, when not whispering sweet nothings into my ear over the gunwale? First and foremost, he would always stay calm. Be prepared for anything, and don't let the enemy see you're frightened.

Whoever had dared to climb aboard the boat obviously had no idea there was a southern belle about, specially one who was armed not only with the good captain's rules of engagement but a heavy onyx table lamp in her hand. I crept silently up the stairs where Larry and I had once made whoopee, the whir of the engine just about overwhelming the thump of my terrified beating heart.

When I stepped outside, I could see the outline of a large man leaning against the tiller. I lifted the lamp high in my right hand and then brought it down with as much force as I could muster on his head. It made an almighty crack and I knew I'd whomped him good and proper, but he stayed on his feet. In fact he whipped around to see who it was who'd just tried to flatten his hairstyle.

It was Larry.

'Caro – what the hell...' he started saying.

'Oooops,' I said, just as he collapsed into an ungainly heap.

Well, they say you always hurt the one you love.

CHAPTER NINE

What in sweet Aunt Pattypan's sack of old socks was I thinking of? I'd only gone and killed the only man I'd ever truly loved. And whereas a judge might consider that murdering one man was a touch unfortunate, two was just plain mean. Exactly how many murders do you have to rack up before you officially become a serial killer? I wouldn't have thought two was quite enough, although it seemed like a pretty good start.

'Wake up Larry,' I said, slapping him in the face in a desperate attempt to bring him round. 'Wake up, goddam it!'

Still he remained unresponsive. Had he already gone to a better place? I didn't like to call it heaven as it could never be that without the two of us there, together.

But thank god, just as I was wondering if it was once again time to flee the scene of the crime, he groaned and sat up, gingerly placing his hand on his head to check the damage.

'What in heaven's name did you do that for?' he said. 'You're not still bitter about us breaking up, are you?'

'As if,' I lied. 'I'm so over that.'

'If you say so.'

'Haven't you heard? I'm on a murder spree. First a Russian guy I picked up at a showbusiness party, today you, and next it'll be that guy who patrols the canal side. After that, the Lord only knows.'

'Ouch, it really hurts,' he said.

'I'm real sorry. But why do all serial killers have to be men, anyway? I'm striking a new blow for feminism – the first female mass murderer.'

'Well, you're not very good at it. I'd stick to presenting radio, if I were you.'

Looking at him, I had to admit he was still handsome, in an older guy kind of way.

'Here, let me take a look at that first,' I said. 'Where do you keep your first aid box?'

He pointed me in the direction of the bedroom, where I grabbed some bandages, a pair of scissors and a bottle of TCP disinfectant.

'Are you feeling swimmy-headed?' I said, going through my medical checklist.

'Come again?' he said. He seemed to have forgotten my southern belle way of talking.

'I mean, are you feeling dizzy?' I said. 'If so, we should get you straight to hospital.' I started rubbing cream on his head.

'Ouch! No need for that. The only reason my head is spinning is because of seeing you again.' The old smoothie. Or maybe he really meant it?

'We'll have none of that malarkey, thank you very much,' I reprimanded him.

'I wouldn't mind you in a nurse's outfit,' he said.

'Been there, hired the costume, for the six o'clock forecast. It's always guaranteed to put the ratings up.'

'I suspect that's not all it puts up,' he said, rather disappointingly.

'I don't seem to remember you being this lewd, Larry. It really doesn't become you, you bein' a middle-aged man an' all.'

'Don't remind me.'

'You needn't think I'm proud of dressing up in provocative costumes. It was just a means to an end so I could afford to buy a house in London.'

'Really? We've got so much to catch up on, Caro.'

'You needn't think I've come all this way for a bit of chit chat. I chose to come here simply as a place to lie low, I was going to be long gone before you got back from your holiday,' I said, not quite telling the complete truth.

'I'm beginning to get the picture,' he said, his spirits noticeably dropping.

'You've got no idea the mess I'm in, Larry. There's a warrant out for my arrest and I've got half of Eastern Europe trying to kill me, but I don't know what I've done to upset them. I reckon it's darn unreasonable of them not to tell me.'

'I've seen plenty of articles in the papers, and on TV. And of course, I've been worried sick about you, but I never thought you'd come looking for my help.'

'It's just a place to hide away. What would you possibly know about international global stuff like this, Larry, you a country-born canal journalist? You'd be way out of your depth. I need somebody who knows what they're talking about on life and death stuff and global conspiracies, not an expert on British inland waterways.'

OK, so I may have been expressing my anger about the break-up of our relationship by other means, whereas he was choosing to rise above it, being all mature and grown-up. That was his way, which is why I liked him in the first place.

'OK, first could I suggest you stay here a little longer, and not to go just because I've arrived on the scene,' he said. 'I can keep out of the way if you would prefer, but this is no time to put yourself at risk by going back out there again all because of something that happened between me and you in the past.' His usual good sense. How annoying!

'So you ain't gonna hand me into the cops?'

'How could you possibly think I'd do that?' he asked, looking a little hurt.

'I bet your wife would, though,' I couldn't help but suggest.

'Good enough reason for me to say nothing to her about you being here.'

'And no other reason than that?'

'No other reason whatsoever,' he said emphatically.

Now there spoke a real, mature man, with strong arms and a wide, manly back. Was it any wonder I used to fancy the pants off him?

'But just before we go any further,' he asked as I prepared myself for the worst, 'Why did you decide to club me on the head?'

'I figured you were an intruder. And I never meant to hurt you that bad,' I tried to explain.

'And that's supposed to make me feel better?'

'It could have been much worse, Larry. Remember I used to be a recruit in the Atlanta Defense Volunteer Force and I've been trained to kill a man with my bare hands.'

'How could I forget?' he said, smiling.

'You see, I met this interfering guy on the tow path,' I explained.

'Ah, that would be Andy.'

'He said you wouldn't get back until Wednesday, and that criminals had been stealing narrowboats, so I put two and two together and figured you must be a thief –

either that, or you were one of those hired killers, or the cops. What was a girl sp'osed to do?'

'It's beginning to make sense – although I do stress, only beginning.'

'And this Andy, when he wasn't talking about canal boat thieves, he was rabbitin' on about 'Larry's girls' and how they were always visiting your boat.' Larry gave a deep sigh. 'Not that it's any of my business,' I quickly added.

'He's a retired tax inspector who's got too much time on his hands, Caro. He's always looking for scandal where there is none.'

'I should never have raised the subject.'

'I occasionally get requests from university students reading Geography to take a look around my boat, simple as that.'

'But always from girls, he said.'

'There was a young man here only just the other week.'

'As I said, none of my flipping business,' I reminded him, but I was feeling better for the explanation all the same.

He didn't kiss me goodbye, which was probably just as well, although a little disappointing. He promised to keep an eye out for me night and day, without saying a word to anybody else. So, what of my situation? I guess I should really prioritize being on the run from the law and the lawless, but in my world human feelings come first, so let's talk about Larry. OK, so he'd put on a few extra pounds here and there, and the hairline had receded a little further than I recalled it, but no matter how hard I tried to dismiss him as a tired old man who lived in fear of his wife, he still made my heart skip a beat. I'd hidden in his boat, but he still floated mine, and when I heard his deep manly voice and eyed his strong muscular arms you don't need telling that I was all of a tingle.

In truth, it wouldn't have taken too much to get me back into his hammock – but for what? Brilliant super-hot sex notwithstanding, of course. He was never going to leave his wife for me, however great the rumpy pumpy, so what was the point except for a brief shot of instant pleasure?

So, meet the new Miss Caro. No longer living for the moment but a gal with an eye for the future and the kind of man she could create a life with. I guess it happens to us all, eventually.

Plus, I could see Larry was striving so hard not to be led astray by my unexpected arrival, in spite of his saucy little innuendos – just his way of coping with so much sexual history suddenly materializing in his cabin. He'd clearly made a decision to stay with his wife, regardless that I'd rocked up from nowhere, and now I must learn to accept it and respect it. Trouble was, I still had those intense feelings of desire swirling around my body, and I couldn't help but think I could influence him to join me on the slippery slope to meaningless sex, if I wanted to. As usual, it all depended on the woman.

So, what of the law and the lawless who were both pursuing me in a race to see who could get to me first? Larry reckoned that on reflection it would be better if I made sure that it was the police who won the race, in view of the murderous intent of the Russians, who definitely wanted me dead. Forever Mr. Sensible, although not exactly romantic, was it, agreeing to have me locked up in a police cell when I'd done nothing wrong? Yet when push came to shove, something told me he was talking sense, because he was a grown-up who thought stuff through, whereas I let my feelings rule the roost.

A shame he couldn't have been as clear-headed when he let me down all those years ago after proposing marriage to me at my wedding . What would Mr. Sensible have to say about that particular can of worms? Not that I suspected he wanted to talk about it. You can bet your sweet bippy he didn't, although he was more than happy to ramble on about how the Russian Ambassador had been called in to see our Foreign Secretary in the wake of Vlad being murdered. But then he suddenly went all nostalgic on me, romantically recalling our first few meetings in the Bush pub, and how the landlady there thought we looked good together.

'That's all very well Larry, but if everything was as hunky dory as you suggest, why did you decide to dump me?'

I couldn't help feeling like the woman who'd broken wind during the eulogy at a funeral. At least Larry appeared suitably embarrassed.

'I'm not sure it's such a good idea for us to go raking over our past,' was the best he could offer in response.

'Then let me answer for you. You didn't want to hurt your children, and you felt obliged to stay with your wife, plus you wanted to see your kids through school, because you love them dearly. Am I close?'

'All those things were important,' he admitted.

'I need to know more Larry, otherwise it's Groundhog Day for me, stuck in the same groove forever,' I said. He just paced around the cabin, mumbling that it wasn't easy for him to explain.

'You can only imagine how your decision affected me. It left me unable to commit to a meaningful relationship if I met a guy who was looking for something more long-term,' I explained.

'OK, it's like this,' he said. 'When I proposed to you at your wedding after Stan had so cruelly stood you up at the altar, I meant every word of it – at first.'

'So, you proposed to me on a whim, or outta pity maybe?'

'No, but it was only after I proposed that I reflected on how perfect our relationship had been, and I realised that getting married could ruin it. I know only too well all the compromises you have to make in a marriage. I'd be watching the magic fade as we drifted apart. And I just couldn't face it, Caro.'

'And I had you down as an optimist.'

'An optimist, no, but a realist, yes. Better for Larry and Caro to be a glorious memory than a tragic reality. That was the way I saw it.'

'I see,' I said. I'd never felt more confused in my life.

'But I never stopped loving you, Caro, and I never will,' he said.

CHAPTER TEN

Having chewed over the fat and then spat it out, I figured
that if Larry hadn't got the courage to get married because
of some weird concept of perfection, then he wasn't the
man I'd figured he was. He was just another dumb old
romantic fool. He claimed he'd loved me, and had never
stopped, if he was to be believed, which in some strange
roundabout way meant I could finally let him go without
recrimination or malice. I knew that at least his heart
had been true, even if it had lacked the strength to see it
through to the end.

It was time to get over it, I told myself, and it seemed
that now we both had. A huge load had been lifted from
our shoulders as we had become more relaxed together,

chatting away about anything and everything that came into our heads.

I gave him a slightly censored version of how Inspector Flowers had come into my life, how he'd moved into my apartment to offer protection after a break in, and how he would have been totally convinced of my innocence, having spent time with me keeping me safe.

'You should hand yourself over to him, and then he could offer you a place of safety until he has been able to prove your innocence,' Larry advised. It always seemed so obvious when he said it.

The contents of the memory stick given to me by Vlad for safe keeping were beyond even him. We struggled to make any kind of sense at all of those algorithms and equations on the PC screen. We really needed to raise our game and enlist the help of some experts who might know what the hell they were talking about, which is why, with Larry's full support, I texted Inspector Flowers, offering to meet him under the clock at Waterloo Station the very next evening.

'Where are you?' he instantly replied. Still, he cared about me, but I refused to give him my location or say any more until we touched base the following night.

So, that left Larry and me on our last night together. I decided to dress to impress to remind Larry of what he'd be missing in the miserable years ahead of him. Call me vengeful if you must, but a southern belle does enjoys dressing sassy.

I put on a tight-fitting pink silk blouse which complemented my figure-hugging grey pencil skirt and sexy stilettoes. When he saw me in all my finery, he winced as if the sight was a physical blow.

We had intended to slip away to the nearest pub under cover of darkness, but after drinking several glasses of Olaf's extra strong vodka we seemed to lose the will to abandon ship. Instead we made fun of one another's accents, me with my southern drawl, and him with his Midlands drone.

Now that we'd relaxed following our previous impasse and the booze began to weave its mischievous magic spell, there were no longer any barriers between us.

'Our audience research conclusively proves that guys just lurve the way I speak,' I told him. 'They find it real sexy.'

'You don't say,' he said. 'I can't say I've ever noticed.'

'Well let me try whispering something in your ear – that always used to do the trick.'

'OK, but I can't be held responsible for my actions,' he replied.

'Last night, I dreamt I was sucking your...' Well that didn't take long. I was going to say toes, but he'd already jumped to his own conclusions and he came on strong, primed to ravish me. And I felt I'd been designed to be ravished by him, held in those strong arms of his and feeling the warmth of him, the power of him, the sheer balls of him. If this was to be our last fond farewell, then what harm could it possibly do? And the fact that we'd both yearned for each other and tried so hard to resist made it all the more fabulous when it eventually happened. It was just like back in the day, when Larry first fucked me as Stan lay sleeping next door. It was just like old times, kissing one another backwards and forwards like lip tennis. It was love all. He still had the knack of making me feel heavenly and loved and desired and wanton and shameless, all at the same time, and every kiss was sweeter than the last.

You don't have to take your clothes off to have fun, but it really helps, if you want to get well and truly ravished. Larry undid the buttons on my blouse, then unclipped my bra so he could lay those massive hands of his on my boobs and make my nipples tingle with delight.

'How I've missed your breasts,' he said after finally coming up for air.

'And how they've missed having you,' I replied. 'Nobody sucks them better. Now it's my turn.'

I used to think 'open wide' had something to do with going to the dentist until I met Larry. I knelt down and unzipped his pants, eager to liberate that wonderful manhood of his, and taking my favourite lollipop back to where it belonged. How I loved giving him head. It's no chore for this southern belle, not when it's Larry's I'm enjoying.

'How I've missed that cock of yours,' I attempted to say.

'It's rude to talk with your mouth full,' he replied.

And it was, extremely full, and as rude as it gets. But it wasn't all about him, or me, just us.

'How I've missed that tongue of yours,' I said, as he re-familiarised himself with my lady garden, loving my love button better than a whole squad of NFL Players could manage back in my days as a cheerleader for the Atlanta Falcons. But that's another story.

I could barely catch my breath when his great dome entered my compliant sky, and in case you're wondering, yes he did take me from behind on those steps, just for old times' sake, not before ravishing one another on almost every imaginable part of the boat, no doubt to test its water worthiness, and as a fit and proper place to have sex.

To say that Larry had lost none of his spark would be to say that Donald Trump was quite a controversial US President. And if you reckon I've gone yakking on too much about the ins and outs of what happened between Larry and me between the sheets second time around, then in what other way could I possibly impart, how what should have been a fond farewell became a here we go again? I rest my case, and my Gucci handbag too.

So we had great sex, and for Larry it was a game changer. He claimed he was willing to turn his life inside out and leave his wife and children, all because we had great sex, whereas for me – yes, we had great sex, but was that reason enough to devote my life to a guy who believed it had to be perfect, when I knew perfect wasn't always possible? Sure, I loved to be ravished all over the shop, and in as many different positions as is comfortably possible, and consensually manhandled when the occasion demands it, but there again, there would be times when all I wanted was a good book, a nice cup of tea, and a goodnight kiss at bedtime, and then roll over and go to sleep, possibly more often than not. Would that be perfect enough for him, even though he was so much older than me? And would seeing me without my make-up, rushing to the bathroom, feeling miserable, yakking on about nothing – how would that rate on Larry's scale of marital perfection? Not very high!

Sure, he still made my heart flutter, and yes, I loved all those old-fashioned masculine values of his – I would never have to tell him to man up – and yes, I still loved him – so what was the bug in the ointment? Maybe it was because he was no longer forbidden fruit. Was that what really got me off? And what sort of future could I have with a predilection like that? It would be more like a curse. And suddenly I would feel guilty about destroying his family for the sake of our so-called happiness. How selfish was that?

'But we both agreed that we were going to move on,' I reminded him.

'That was then, this was now. I'm leaving her,' he said without a moment's hesitation as he put his pants back on and buttoned up his shirt.

'But you said that before, and look what happened then,' I replied, slipping on my stockings and high heels.

'This time it's different, Caro. The kids are that much older now and they should be able to handle it better, and Ellen is still young enough to start a new life with someone who really loves her.'

'But you and I, Larry – it might be marvelous, but it won't always be perfect.'

'Perfect is for angels. Marvelous is good enough for humans, don't you think?'

I guess that was progress, of a kind. I would just have to ride along on the wave of his enthusiasm, except this time he really would have to drop that bombshell on his wife. However destructive and whatever the pain, there could be no turning back. Truly, we weren't playing at being Larry and Caro anymore – now it was for real.

OK, so that's the relationship sorted – I wish! Now I had an international conspiracy to resolve. All I had to do was to hand over all that global high falutin' stuff to Inspector Flowers, who would bear it on those strong shoulders of his while Larry and I could finally concentrate on being together forever.

It all seemed so simple, back then.

CHAPTER ELEVEN

No matter how much I tried to counsel Larry to consider the consequences of his actions, he was as stubborn as a hog that's being rounded up for the slaughterhouse. He even volunteered to accompany me to see Inspector Flowers, but that was really something I had to do on my own. I didn't want those particular worlds colliding, if you don't mind.

On our way to Birmingham Moor Street Station, where I would catch a train to London, Larry had more plans for our future than a State of the Union address. There was something about how he would sail his boat down south and moor it at Regents Park, just a short walk from where I lived. In spite of all this childlike enthusiasm I struggled to shake off this nagging doubt over whether this particular ship – our relationship – hadn't already sailed. How contrary was I? I would have danced around the kitchen table waving my bloomers in the air only a short while ago at the prospect of getting back with Larry. Yet was it any wonder that I had come over all cautious, considering Larry's history of unfulfilled promises?

'So, when are you going to tell Ellen?' I just had to ask as we weaved our way through the busy morning traffic.

'When the time is right, which will be when you've finally proved your innocence. After all, I wouldn't want to tell my kids that I was leaving their mother for a murderess,' he replied, somewhat insensitively I thought at the time.

I didn't want him hanging around the station like we were trying to recreate a scene from Brief Encounter either, hugging and kissing in his car until we hit the point where we found it hard to let one another go. I was still smitten, just a little more hesitant than Larry, that's all - and why wouldn't I be? Plus, it didn't exactly inspire me with confidence when he warned me not to believe everything I read about us in the newspapers, saying he'd have to downplay our relationship for the sake of foolin' the law, and confusing those heavy hoodlums who wanted me dead.

'But it won't be long before we can come out as a proper couple,' he assured me as he accompanied me out of his vehicle. We embraced on the sidewalk until I cut the kissing short.

'You must tell Ellen,' I warned him, 'because if you don't, I will.'

With those words hopefully ringing in his ears, I was gone, leaving him with a kiss and a threat. I stepped out on to the concourse and the railway station was buzzing with shoppers in search of bargains at the sales, plus a handful of Spurs supporters on their way to a European football tie at Wembley, and most noticeably, a large group of smartly-dressed boys and young men in their neat school uniforms, milling towards what could have been the Hogwarts Express, although it was in fact the 10.55 to London Marylebone via Leamington Spa and High Wycombe.

Maybe I could have been mistaken for an elder sister, or heaven forbid, even one of their mums, coming to wave her darling son off, not a fugitive on the run from the police, but I managed to slip through the crowd without being noticed by the heavy security presence, and climbed aboard the train, while the only attention I got was a few wolf whistles from some of those supposedly well-raised boys.

Once on board, I could feel my sprits lift at the prospect of heading back towards London, where I could continue to pursue my career as a broadcast journalist while creating an open relationship with Larry for all the world to see, once Inspector Flowers had cleared my name.

I snuck into a Business Class carriage, confident

that I could use my southern drawl to beguile the ticket inspector to upgrade my ticket. I particularly wanted to stay away from the eyes of all those prying teenage boys, not wishing to engage with hormonally charged kids.

But then one of them had the nerve to walk into my carriage, and if that wasn't bad enough, he sat directly opposite me, even though there were plenty of seats to go around.

'If you don't mind, would you mind sitting some place else?' I said, barely bothering to look at him as I spoke.

'I can go where I want,' he said with that annoying sense of entitlement so typical of the English public schoolboy.

It wasn't until I lowered my copy of Cosmopolitan, in which I was reading an article on what we can learn from sleeping with other women's husbands, that I finally discovered exactly who I'd been talking to.

'Barry Potter, I do declare,' I said. 'I didn't recognize you in your short trousers.'

'Highly amusing. But I knew exactly who you were in that red wig. Why do you think I sat opposite you?'

'Cos you're missing your mommy, and you thought it would be nice to talk to the pretty lady to stop you feeling so darn lonesome. Am I right?'

He blushed. 'if you carry on talking like that I'll hand you over to the po-leece,' he said, deliberately mocking my accent.

'Don't you dare! And whatever you do, you mustn't mention my name,' I instructed him.

'Of course, you're still most wanted, aren't you, but you'll always be most wanted by me.'

Not bad for a kid, and I couldn't help but notice that he'd been working out too. You should have seen those strong arms of his. Just as well I now had Larry to focus all my carnal desires on. Not that I'm in the habit of ogling teenage boys. You can be certain that as far as I was concerned the best place for Barry Potter was in school, where he well and truly belonged.

'So you're going back to class?' I observed in a condescending tone. 'I spo'se it won't be all bad, catching up with your friends and making out with the sixth form girls.'

'No girls allowed at our school. It's like living in the dark ages. And they wonder why half the boys are gay.'

'Nothing wrong with being gay, Barry Potter,' I admonished him. 'Maybe you should try it sometime.'

'I already have, but it just wasn't me. Loads of the gay guys are straight really, it's just that they make do with boys until they go home for the school holidays and can go with girls. There's nothing wrong with being properly gay, obviously.'

I was kind of glad that he wasn't gay – it would be such a shame for the world of women to miss out on him, even if that wasn't going to include me.

'I can see you've been busy down the gym, Barry. And you're wise for your years, and thoughtful too. Where have you been all my life?' I said, jokingly of course.

'I hadn't been born for most of it,' he replied. Ouch!

'I asked for that, didn't I?' Not that it bothered him as much as it did me.

Just then we were interrupted by a rival member of the Barry Potter fan club, a pretty young dark-haired girl of around his age. 'Where have you been, babes? I've been looking for you everywhere,' she said.

'Can't you see I'm otherwise engaged?' he said, brushing her off like a stray piece of cotton on a jacket. I can't say I wasn't shocked by the way he treated her, but I was a little impressed too.

'Aren't you coming out to play then?' she asked sarcastically.

'I've already told you. There's plenty more boys down the train who will be only too happy for you to give them some company.'

'So, what's with the old lady?' she asked. I didn't first realize she meant me.

'She not an old lady she's a beautiful young woman,' he said, as he sent her on her way. How chivalrous was that? He was more like a shining knight than a young wizard. Some older woman is going to be very lucky, I couldn't help thinking, knowing his predilection for the more mature lady.

'Now that I've found you again, I'm never going to let you go' he said. 'And you being off air is driving me crazy.'

'I'll be back on the show in a few days, once I've

cleared up all the mess, so there will be no need for you to take me home with you,' I explained, attempting to calm him down.

'It wouldn't be the same though, now that I've met you in the flesh,' he said forlornly.

'All it takes for you to be in touch with me is to turn your knob – you know how to do that, don't you? - and I'll be there yakking away,' I promised him.

'That might be ok for the majority of your listeners, Miss Caro, but I need more than that. And you need me too. What with all the trouble you're in, you could do with somebody who knows what they're talking about.'

How sweet of him. And you could tell he really meant it too, even if there may have been an ulterior motive, judging by way he looked longingly at me as the train moved out of the station. It was only natural for a boy of his age, I guess. I buttoned up my blouse, just to leave him in no doubt that I was only available on the radio.

We were still pulling out the station when I heard men's voices down the train and getting nearer all the time – the voices of officialdom. It was a ticket inspector accompanied by a transport policeman, clearly on the lookout for me. In my panic, I even contemplated opening the train door and making a jump for it before the train reached full speed, but they would only catch me, and I would probably end up in a prison hospital with two broken legs.

So, what's a girl sp'osed to do? I'll tell you what I did

do. Just as they got to my seat I flung my arms round Barry and kissed him hard on the lips. I was hoping they would believe we were a loving couple and leave us well alone, which is surely the correct and British thing to do under the circumstances.

Thankfully Barry didn't mind, which is what I'd figured. Anyway he had such darn fine kissing skills that surprisingly, it wasn't a chore.

'Oh, so sorry miss,' said the ticket inspector, obviously a little embarrassed, whereas Barry lay back and took it like a man.

'They don't 'arf start young these days,' I overheard the ticket inspector say as he moved away from us down the train.

'I'm so sorry about that, Barry – it was the only way I could think of hiding from those men,' I explained to him.

'Only too happy to be of assistance, Miss Caro,' he said, moving in to kiss me again.

'You mustn't call me Miss Caro,' I warned him. 'You might give me away.' He was still kissing me. 'Hey Barry honey, we're not doing this for any other reason than trying to put the law off the scent' I said, just in case he thought I actually wanted to kiss him.

'That goes without saying, Miss C,' he said, nuzzling my neck.

'Well, I spo'se they might come looking for us again. Better safe than sorry,' I said. He took me in his strong arms and kissed me some more. He tasted of fresh fruits and spring, whereas Larry had the flavor of the fall about him, although I loved autumn too. Was it any wonder those middle-aged lady friends of his Mom wanted a piece of Barry, shocking though it might seem?

When I heard the voices return, we buried ourselves in one another for safety's sake until they passed. As their voices faded away I became aware of his right hand on my breast, which wasn't part of the deal.

'Now you're being presumptuous again,' I said removing his hand without further ado. I certainly didn't want him to get ideas above his station, which he later told me was Leamington Spa.

'Now let's get one thing straight, Barry Potter. While I was most grateful for you participating in some pretend love play to get me out of a fix, there is no way this is going any further.' I buttoned up my blouse once more.

'And can I ask why?'

'Because I am once again betrothed to another.'

'Oh no, not the old guy on the boat you're always going on about on your radio show?'

'I may have mentioned him once or twice,' I said. I disliked his inference that I was just a one-trick pony as a broadcaster, always banging on about the same old stuff, although I recalled that Olaf had suggested something similar. 'Although I can't say I'm not flattered, to be admired by a handsome young man such as yourself, but you're just a kid Barry, and your future lies elsewhere. I've forgotten more stuff than you will ever know.'

It didn't seem to knock him back. 'Well, if you're so clever and grown-up, what makes you think you can travel around unrecognized just because you're wearing a red wig, when your face has been on every TV news show and internet news page?'

Of course, I appreciated his concern, misdirected though it might be.

'You don't have to worry your pretty little head about it, Barry,' I said, patting him on the knee. 'I have a plan, co-devised by Larry and me. I'm going to hand myself in to Inspector Flowers, because he already knows I'm innocent, having come to my rescue after the first incident in Hampstead.'

He looked at me as if I'd just arrived from another galaxy, while I could see him struggling to find words that would make sense to somebody so obviously less bright than himself.

'Look, I really don't want to rain on your parade, Caro, but I think you'll get banged up long before you hand yourself into Flowers. And who knows what's happened to him? With a name like that I bet he's already been placed on gardening leave, so they can proceed against you without muddying the water.'

'So, what would you advise me to do, o wise one?' I asked.

'Putting the sarcasm to one side, I reckon you still need to lay low for another few weeks, until we can work out why the international conspiracy wants to kill you.'

'That's not what Larry thinks,' I said petulantly.

'And he doesn't think it's anything to do with the weather, having viewed the stuff on Vlad's memory stick – although to be honest, I'm not too sure if he had a clue about the science. He does know an awful lot about canals though,' I said, just in case he was tempted to think my man was some kind of booby.

He unfolded his laptop and fired it up. 'Give it here,' he said. 'Let's see the evidence. Now we'll find out the real reason for everything that's happened to you.'

'You reckon? It's just a bunch of equations and algorithms.'

He gazed at the screen. 'Damn right!' he replied, his eyes practically glowing with excitement.

'Larry reckons it could be something to do with DNA,' I proudly explained.

'Yeah, really clever. It says DNA on a caption at the corner of the frame.' I decided to draw a veil over that.

He began to scroll through the contents of the USB drive. 'This stuff is epoch making, ground breaking, grabbing you by the gonads fucking amazing!' he said, totally gripped by excitement. 'It's some sort of formula for extending human life, or maybe even living forever, if I'm not mistaken. I would like our professor back at school to take a serious look at this, and I daren't email it to him. It's much too top secret to start exposing it to the web.'

'How can you possibly know this stuff, Barry?' I said.

'Fancy working at our crusty old school for a few weeks?'

'Not specially. I already have a job as London's top radio presenter, in case you forgot. I know I nearly did.'

'I don't suppose you would possess any teaching qualifications? Nothing too fancy.'

'Afraid not,' I replied as he continued to type merrily away on his keyboard.

'OK, have you got a female friend who could team up with you? Then we could get rid of those two witches who run our school health centre and hire you two instead.'

'Have you taken leave of your senses, Barry Potter? And it's just plain wrong to get somebody fired through no fault of their own.'

'Trust me Miss C, these women should have been dismissed years ago. When they're not perving at the sixth form boys they're running an illegal trade in cannabis for all the school dopeheads.'

'Well, in that case...' I rather pathetically replied, while he started tip-tapping on his keyboard to make stuff happen.

'There you go – both of them fired. Now we'll just add a little note from you and your friend, whose name is...?'

'Miss Pearl Robinson.'

'...detailing your awesome experience in the area of youth health care, and voila, the job is yours!'

'But I don't have any medical qualifications either.'

'A mere detail. You'll just have to wing it.'

'Look Barry, I'm not so sure this is really a good idea – what will Larry think? And Inspector Flowers is expecting me at Waterloo Station.'

'He's probably planning to arrest you, whereas what I'm offering is a safe place to stay, a new identity, plus paid employment and an esteemed physics professor who will be able to establish once and for all why people want to kill you.'

He truly was something else, I couldn't help reflecting, although I doubted whether Larry would be that sympathetic to my unexpected change of plan. But Barry was no threat to him, was he? It was older guys who boiled my kettle, not kids, because I need a real man to make me really whistle.

But then I was drawn back to how he'd been tutored in the ways of love by some middle-aged lady friends of his mom, who'd had this pass-him-on *thang* going on. I began to wonder whether that's what would have happened in so called primitive times, when a mother might have turned to her female friends to educate her sons in the arts of making love and procreation. It kind of made biological sense.

'You're very confident for a boy so young,' I just had to say.

'That's exactly what mum's friends used to say after I'd seduced them all,' he said, none too modestly.

'Are you sure it wasn't the other way around?'

'No way – apart from the first one. She climbed into my bed one Christmas Eve, saying that she had a very special present to give me. The same thing happened every night over the holiday period until I'd taken her from every conceivable position. I couldn't have been more grateful for her patience and good humor, although she was delighted with me too. That's when she started waxing lyrical about me to her best friend, so I was passed on further down the MILF line, one by one, until I'd satisfied them all.'

'It sure as hell beats old Sandy Claus when your Mom has friends like that! But don't go thinkin' I'm approvin.' You should have been writing your thank-you letters to your uncles and aunts instead. Twelve days of Christmas indeed!'

We'd taken our eye off the ball, talking about stuff that was probably best left forgotten. Just then the train came to a juddering halt in the middle of nowhere, alongside a field where cows grazed. In the silence we heard the sound of more police officers coming our way,

'Time to disembark Miss C, before you get caught,' said Barry.

'They've gone into lockdown, unless I can access the code to open the train door,' Barry explained quite calmly.

'Open Sesame,' he said, and the door rumbled open at his command. Wasn't there anything this young man couldn't achieve?

'Are you by any chance related to James Bond? Perhaps he's your uncle,' I asked.

'Sadly, like Harry Potter, and all the best people in England, he doesn't really exist. Now go,' he instructed me.

'Where to?' I replied, looking down at the embankment below me.

'To Saint Drogo's Boarding School for the Sons of Gentlefolk, about ten miles from here between Leamington Spa and Banbury, where you can liaise with your friend and report for duty at 2 pm.'

'Won't they want some kind of references, security checks?'

'Already done on line – fake references and resumé. Now jump!'

And perhaps foolishly, I did as he commanded, case in hand, as the doors closed behind me. I hid in the undergrowth until the train pulled away some ten minutes later. Maybe I should never have listened to Barry Potter, although it seemed like I wasn't the first woman to have first thought that, and others clearly reckoned he was just what the doctor ordered.

CHAPTER TWELVE

Needless to say, Barry had thought of everything. He had booked me into what he described as a discreet guest house in Leamington Spa, and I was welcomed there by a rather brassy landlady, who obviously knew him and had a soft spot for him. 'Oh yes, young Mr Potter. We all love a bit of Barry, don't we?' she said. She was dressed as if she was in the Last Chance Saloon, revealing a touch too much cleavage and wearing far too much make-up for a woman of her years.

'We don't ask no questions here, lovey,' she said. That would suit me just fine, given the predicament I was in. 'And when will young Mr Potter be joining you?' she asked, tapping the side of her nose with a knowing air.

'He won't,' I said rather too firmly. 'He should be back at school by now.'

'I don't judge,' she replied, which made me feel worse than if she did.

'Why would I?' she went on. 'I've entertained him myself, when one of his polite respectable middle-aged ladies lost her nerve and failed to show. Well, it's a shame to see a freshly made bed go to waste.'

Far too much information, I yearned to yell, but she obviously thought I was singing from the same hymn sheet as her and wanted to tell me more.

'He's ruddy unbelievable in bed. The best you'll find round these parts – and what parts, if you get my drift. You won't regret it my dear.'

Barry Potter, how could you? I would admonish him when I next saw him in school. He wasn't much better than a gigolo – and that's only a fancy foreign word for a male prostitute who's paid to please women. Did he see me in the same light as this dreadful landlady, who was little more than a madam in a brothel for ladies, or was I better than that? Lord only knows.

'Of course, I can see you're a few years younger than most of Barry's ladies, but still old enough to know better, eh?' she said, nudging me in the ribs.

'I can assure you, my interest in Barry is purely platonic. We're not even good friends.'

'More fool you,' she said as she handed me my room keys. 'I've had quite a few sixth form students in my time – my husband can't get it up anymore. I reckon it must be something to do with the water. But I've never experienced anything like Barry Potter. And you're talking to a woman who had Tom Jones in his prime, on a one-night stand in a Ford Cortina just outside Pontypridd, where he serenaded me with The Green Green Grass Of Home while I gave him a blow job.'

'It's not unusual,' I couldn't stop myself from saying.

I could see that Barry needed protecting from the ravenous cougars he'd surrounded himself with, and I was the woman to do it. I would instruct him to aspire to higher things, and teach him there was more to life than chasing after middle-aged women who should know better than to rob a boy of his boyhood. And by helping me on my quest to rid the world of evil Russian agents he would have something else to think about – something more noble and uplifting than a MILF's last hurrah. Or were they no more than typical females like me, with healthy sexual appetites, who refused to go quietly, unlike their limply inadequate husbands who just couldn't rise to the occasion? And was it all due to all those female hormones sloshing around in the sea? On behalf of women everywhere, I must remember to tell Barry not to go swimming at the seaside.

I do declare that all this talk of Barry Potter and his remarkable proclivities had worked its way into my dreams, where I wasn't really sure I wanted it to be. I was seeing visions of him naked with those friends of his mom, entirely unsuitable for a southern belle like me, when I would rather be dreaming of kittens and rabbits in springtime, and Larry of course.

When I picked up a copy of the *Coventry Evening Telegraph* the next day, all thoughts of Barry went from my mind. It had a picture of Larry on the front page. He was being quoted as saying how shocked he was to discover that the Killer In High Heels had been hiding on his boat without him knowing. 'It made me feel sick to my stomach to find that a woman who could kill a man in cold blood had sought sanctuary in my boat,' he had apparently said, alongside a picture of him on the towpath looking like a man who was losing his religion. 'I had no idea this girl had illegally broken in and had been living there. It's people like her who give canal boating a bad name.'

Just as well he'd warned me something like this might appear, although it didn't make it any easier. I would have to live with it – just as long as he told his wife pretty darn soon.

At least I was looking forward to meeting Pearl as I headed towards Leamington Spa Station. I'd tried to explain to her by text what had been going on, but had failed miserably. Talk about complicated! She seemed to grasp that we would be working together in the health centre at a boy's public school, but didn't quite understand why, or how, or what for. Trouble was, neither did I. She would have to speak to Barry on that one, when she wasn't pouring out her heart to Olaf, who had been calling round to see her at our house in Hampstead, to keep her updated of my progress so far. And it seems they had really been hitting it off. I wondered whether there might be a little romance in the air, in between partaking of vodka and pickled sausages.

As I waited on the appropriate platform for the London train to arrive, I could hear a strangulated Polish voice shouting in the distance - Olaf. And then I heard Pearl too. 'Over here, you beautiful cow!' I heard him shout from outside the station concourse. 'We're here for you', Pearl joined in. That confused me, as I'd been expecting her to arrive on the 9.35 from London Marylebone, and not in a ten-wheel truck parked across half a dozen quick drop-off bays.

'You're looking fine, girlfriend,' I said as I watched her climb elegantly out of the cab, I knew a boob job when I saw one – she was looking even more feminine than I remembered her.

'You too,' she said, giving me a high five. 'Now what is it you want me to do – work in a Health Centre?'

'I'd best let Barry Potter explain that one to you.'

'Barry Potter?'

'He's a boy wonder I met on a train. He dreamed up a plan to get me out of my hole,' I said.

'So, you've knocked Larry on the head?'

'Literally in fact, but we're still together in spite of that. He's going to tell his wife, then sail his boat down to

London where we can live happily ever after.'

'But what about those crazy guys who want you dead?'

'That's where Barry Potter comes in, and his friend the Professor at Saint Drongo's School.'

'Of course it is,' she said. Olaf invited us to climb back in, concerned that he might be fined if we didn't get moving pretty darn soon.

'Hey Caro,' said Olaf the ever faithful, 'I'm here for you baby. Do you like Pearl's new tits?'

'I love them, but not quite as much as you do, I suspect,' I replied. He fired up his truck to head off in the direction of Saint Drongo's Academy for the Sons of Gentlefolk, where Barry would be waiting for us, and all would become clear.

'Why you leave ship?' Olaf enquired as we thundered through the leafy Warwickshire lanes.

'Having made it up with Larry, I was on my way to hand myself into Inspector Flowers – both Larry and I agreed it was the right thing to do – but then I was hijacked by a teenage boy on a train.'

'I don't get it,' said Olaf.

'You've always been more partial to the older man,' said Pearl.

'It's not what you're thinking, there's nothing going on between Barry and me. I'm surprised you would even suggest such a thing. Watch that pheasant!' I yelled as Olaf swerved to try to get himself some roadkill. 'No, he's a kind of boy genius who reckons he can get to the bottom of why guys have been trying to kill me. And not only that – there's a professor at his school who should be able to decipher the DNA code they're all trying to get their hands on.'

Olaf gave a blast of approval on his horn, making an oncoming motorist almost swerve off into a ditch.

'I can't wait to catch that show when Caro comes back in triumph,' said Olaf. 'We can prove you're a good girl after all, and save the world while we're at it – but first, here's a few messages from our sponsors.'

You couldn't fault his devotion to our show.

It didn't take long to reach Barry's school, which was hardly surprising considering the ridiculous speed Olaf drove at. A great gothic pile came looming into view.

'Oh god, it's like that crazy place where silly boys and girls play hockey in the sky,' Olaf observed.

'Yep, Hogwarts here we come,' I proclaimed, climbing out of Olaf's cab. Pearl kissed him meaningfully on the lips in what looked like a surprisingly fond farewell, which got me wondering. We descended down the steps of the gigantic truck, observed by a man who I presumed to be the janitor, or caretaker as they say over here. Not the traditional way to make your entrance at one of the great public schools of England.

'Can I help you, laydees?' he said in the slightly nauseating way a certain kind of man pronounces that word, with overtones of unwelcome sexual interest and an ill-judged sense of entitlement over women.

'Reporting for duty at the Young Men's Sanitorium, sir!' I said with a mock military salute. I was keen not to betray any sense of my real feeling – what in God's green earth were Pearl and I doing there?

'Oh, are you now?' he said. 'There'll be ructions in the dormitories when the young gentlemen see the delightful young laydees who have come to tend their aches and pains, not to mention their unmentionables.'

'Then don't mention them – I know we certainly won't,' I said, putting him right straight away.

'I can see them now once they get a shufty of you two little crackers, queueing up outside the sanitorium door with their mystery illnesses. Let's face it, your predecessors weren't exactly lookers. You two will certainly stir up those adolescent hormones, not that they need much stirring, if you get my drift.'

I had dragged Pearl all the way over here for this?

'No, I don't – nor do I want to,' I replied.

'Don't get me wrong – I'm sure you are both extremely upright, clean living laydees...' In spite of arriving at school like a couple of truck stop hookers, was what he wanted to say. '...but who would have guessed, Jess and Linda fired for peddling drugs through the sanitorium. Just as well they completed the annual medical examinations of the young gentlemen before they were dismissed.'

'Isn't it just,' I heartily agreed.

'Except for the sixth formers,' he added. 'Linda always used to joke that they kept the best to last.'

Did I just see the hint of a smirk on Pearl's face? I could have slapped her. And as for this caretaker – maybe I could persuade Barry to get him fired and replaced by Tom Hardy? I wouldn't mind inspecting him.

The caretaker escorted us into the school, still going on about how our presence would inflame the young gentlemen. We were only two people on a staff of over 100, so what was the big deal? We were women – get over it, I wanted to say, but I chose to smile sweetly instead.

'There are your rooms. I can keep a close eye on you girls from over the way,' said the caretaker with a wink. He was getting creepier by the minute. Fortunately he was then called away in a hurry – apparently a leak had been reported in the gentleman's toilets. Did they even have ladies' rest rooms around here?

'Do you want to scream first or shall I?' said Pearl when we got inside my room. There was a letter waiting for us from the Head, Mr Royston Verney, MA Lit, officially welcoming us to the school.

'Rule One – we're not conducting any medical examinations on the students,' I said, laying down the law to Pearl.

'If you say so,' she replied.

'We could get sent down for years if they found out we're not qualified to do the job. And Rule Two – when in doubt, we refer our patients to the doctors or the hospital. Nobody's going to die on our watch. And if they're malingering, we hand out paracetamol.'

Pearl accepted the terms and conditions before retiring to her room to unpack and freshen up. But no sooner had she gone than there was a knock at the door, as if someone had been waiting until I was alone. It was Barry.

'Mr Potter, I do declare. What have you got us into?' I said with a mixture of exasperation at where we found ourselves and relief to see him again.

'Everything is going to be fine,' he replied. As if he really knew.

'You shouldn't be here, knocking at my door. The caretaker's keeping a watch on our rooms.'

'Don't worry about him – the man's a plonker. I arranged for that leak to get him out of the way.'

'Now why doesn't that surprise me? Is there anything you can't control?'

'You,' he said, confidently stepping inside my room.

'Apparently, we've got to give the sixth formers their medical examination,' I said. 'How in Trump are we s'posed to do that?'

'There's nothing to it. You just walk down a row of students ticking boxes on a form to confirm that they've all got two arms, two legs and one head,' he said.

'It's not those particular bits I'm worried about.'

'Nothing you haven't seen before, Miss Caro,' he said, smirking.

'So, now what? You got us into this mess, now get us out of it.'

'Well, we could carry on where we left off in the train, kissing and cuddling, or alternatively, I could get your memory stick to the Professor and get it analyzed.'

'Get the Professor up to speed, if you please. The sooner Miss Pearl and I are out of here, the better.'

'But not before you've addressed the school to outline your new health care policy."

'And what in Hans Christian Andersen am I sp'osed to say?'

'You could try wrap up warm, take plenty of exercise and go easy on the wanking,' he suggested, then disappeared before the caretaker reappeared.

The caretaker might have been a pain, but we were far more impressed with the headmaster, especially Pearl, when we met him over breakfast the next day prior to school assembly.

'Let me say what a delight it is to have you two medical professionals on board to minister in the treatment of ailments,' he said, welcoming us. How charming to be greeted by a real gentleman.

'Only too glad to be of service,' said Pearl, fluttering her now extravagant false eyelashes at him. And I thought she was sweet on Olaf.

'You remind me of that Jacob Rees Mogg,' she said, as bold as one of her recently-acquired push-up bras. 'Are you married?'

'I think I'm what's called not the marrying kind,' he replied. Pearl and I shared a knowing look. 'Or maybe

I'm really married to my profession, and my students are the sons I never had.'

'Aw, isn't he sweet,' said Pearl, clearly doting on this 21st Century Mr Chips.

'Maybe you haven't just met the right person yet,' said Pearl. She might as well have been shouting, 'Me me me!'

'Oh, I don't think anybody's going to be interested in a fusty old chap like me.'

'You might be surprised. And you're not that old either, and not so much fusty as retro,' she said. I felt like a total gooseberry.

'And have you any proposals as to how we can improve the health of our young men, Miss Caro?' he said, addressing me in my capacity of Head Nurse.

'You could start by admitting girls – to the sixth form first if needs be – to create a more balanced community, and a few more female teachers might be beneficial too.'

'Well, the all-male staff was very much the idea of my predecessor, Mr Williams, who preferred to surround himself with rugby-playing types, almost regardless of their academic qualifications. Personally I agree, we need to balance things up a bit.'

'Even Hogwarts takes girl pupils, if JK Rowling is to be believed,' said Pearl.

'So I hear,' said Royston.' However we are governed by a charter which stipulates that we are only allowed to admit boys.' He seemed genuinely sorry about it.

'Just imagine, Royston,' said Pearl, helping him to

butter his crumpet. 'You could be the headmaster who goes down in history as the man who dragged Saint Drongo's into the 21st Century by tearing up the Charter and finally admitting girls.'

'Do you know what, you've fired me up,' said the Head to us both. 'I'll get to work on it straight away. You ladies will need to be on standby for the annual staff rugby match, ready to treat the inevitable casualties. It kicks off later today. And don't forget, the yearly health inspection for the Sixth Form is also long overdue.'

'We've certainly got our hands full, Headmaster,' said Pearl.

'Haven't we just,' I concurred, giving her a meaningful glare.

After breakfast we processed towards the Grand Hall with other staff members, the majority of whom looked like paid-up members of the Rugby first fifteen. I really wasn't sure whether this was a good environment for a betrothed woman like myself, with all those hunky athletic specimens who had been denied female company for so long. They behaved as if we had been placed in school purely for their benefit – talk about a sense of entitlement.

At the back of the hall, where I assumed the Professor might hang out, sat a small group of more elderly teachers. To hell with the hunks – this was the guy who could set me free. I smiled sweetly at them, hoping to meet the esteemed academic soon.

The Headmaster, or Royston, as he invited us to call him, asked us to stand either side of him at the front of the stage, with all the hunks and the aged ones lined up behind us. And then Pearl had the barefaced cheek to link arms with Royston – so I wasn't going to be left out, flanked either side by his bitches from the sanitorium, or that's how the boys must have seen us. Having given me a glowing introduction – although I'm not sure quite what for – the Head invited me to speak to the school, which included all those extremely fit teachers, and Barry Potter urging me on.

Most women couldn't tell you what it's like to be facing a hall full of over 1,000 young men, most of them sporting erections, but I sure can.

'I can see you're all standing to attention. At ease,' I said, trying to lighten the mood a little. 'Come on, it's rude to point – okay, if that's the way you want to play it. Is this what they call a standing ovation.?' That got me my first laugh, and it was all downhill from there on. It guaranteed a great turn out on our first day of business at the Sanitorium, with boys in line right around the block. And who should be at the front of the line, but Barry Potter – I bet he'd manipulated something or other to get pole position.

I asked Pearl to go and tidy up the medicine cupboard so I could consult Barry on my own, given the sensitivity of our situation together. But when I walked into the examination area there was Barry, busily engaged in getting naked, when I hadn't even asked him to take his tie off.

'What do you think you're darn well doing?' I challenged him.

'I'm behaving as one does when having a medical check-up,' he said arrogantly. 'So, what do you reckon?' he twirled around in his packed Calvin Kleins.

'Please put it away,' I replied, which took some of the wind out of his sails. 'OK, so what news of the Professor?' I enquired.

'A minor hiccup to report,' he said.

'Sounds ominous. If you've brought me all this way just so I can see you lying there like some Greek god on the examination table, you've got another think coming.'

'I forgot to say there's a conference on nuclear thermodynamics that the Prof's been invited to attend in Bristol, but don't worry, he'll be back within the week.'

'Oh great, that's all I need to hear. What with the sixth form examination coming up and the staff rugby match, I really don't think this place is good for me, Barry.'

'Don't worry, you went down a storm at Morning Assembly,' he said, swinging his legs back over the table to get dressed.

'It's so nice to be appreciated.'

Having awarded Barry a clean bill of health, I sent him back to his class. 'It's all in good working order!' I shouted after him down the corridor, loud enough to embarrass him in front of his friends.

That was more than I could say for our second patient of the day, a boy unpromisingly called Winkle, who asked me to rub some ointment into his coccyx. In your dreams Mr. Winkle, not that I could locate a coccyx, even if I wanted to. Now there's a sentence I never expected to write.

I needed to wise up, being a nurse as best as I could by studying medical health manuals and occasionally going on line to check stuff out, while Pearl spent some more quality time with Royston to discuss her plans for a room where the transgender boys could have a safe place to be themselves. So I headed off to the staff rugby match unaccompanied, and found myself forced to watch hordes of fit young men kicking seven bells out of one another. I patched the injured ones up as they came off and gave them a little TLC before returning them to the fray. And I was getting paid for it.

After the game had finished I accidentally took the wrong door and walked into their dressing room, where I was confronted by more gorgeous men than you could imagine in a full-blown female fantasy. I didn't know where to look for fear of going cross-eyed, but the players carried on towelling themselves down regardless.

'Sorry guys, I took a wrong turning,' I explained as I walked down the naked guard of honor they gave me and disappeared into the steam. Here I inexplicably finished up in the arms of the beautiful dark-skinned young man who had played prop forward, and his right wingback joined us, with me as the filling in their sandwich. I just closed my eyes and breathed it all in. The others didn't want to be left out, either, and I soon found myself surrounded by young manly muscles on all sides. But it was just hugs you understand, so technically nothing that could be considered being unfaithful to Larry, although maybe I wouldn't be telling him about this fandango in a bath house. He might get the wrong end of the stick, whereas I only got the right end. But the less said about that the better.

Of course, I should have found my way out of there quicker, but when a fantasy comes true and is handed to a lady on a plate, what's that lady sp'osed to do? You could say I'd had a West Country moment, a relapse if you will, so I would do what any self-respecting southern belle would do after she's fallen off her stallion, and that's to climb right back on again. Lord only knows what Larry would think if he ever found out. That will teach him to disown me in the local paper, I couldn't help myself thinking. And what he didn't know wouldn't hurt him. After all, it was just a bit of harmless fun, wasn't it?

Word soon spread around the school about my unfortunate error. Barry simply smiled when he heard my lame explanation for ending up in the men's changing room. Pearl wouldn't let it rest, convinced that I'd made a deliberate mistake, but I would tease her about her taking walks with Royston in the school grounds together and looking dreamily into one another's eyes. He claimed never to have had that much interest in women until he met Pearl.

'Royston reckons I'm not like other girls,' Pearl explained.

'He's not wrong there,' I replied. 'When are you going to tell him you weren't born a girl?'

'Soon,' she replied, 'although I'm not expecting there to be a problem. In fact, it could even work out to be an advantage.' Too much information.

We were in danger of getting sidetracked with her relentless pursuit of Royston and my half-hearted, passing interest in Barry, but not in a sexual way. I could have hugged him, however, when he told me that the Professor had just returned from his conference and was already examining the contents of our memory stick.

'Well, butter my butt and call me a biscuit!' I cried out in delight. I was exhilarated by the prospect of getting out of that place. But first I had to be briefed by Barry on how to handle the Professor and his somewhat unusual manner. He wasn't one for small talk apparently, with so many hang-ups , having made some bad choices in life. He had appeared on the Halloween Edition of Pointless dressed as Frank N' Furter from the Rocky Horror Show wearing a basque and suspenders, much to the consternation of his superiors at the Home Office. That was something you were only supposed to do at home.

'That's why he finished up here at Saint Drongo's, instead of occupying one of the most senior scientific positions in the land,' Barry explained. 'And he's pretty sore about it, because he says it was just a bit of harmless fun. So what if he was a sweet transvestite from Transylvania?'

Barry rated him highly though, as the Professor had taken him under his wing, becoming something of a substitute father for his dad, who lived in Kenya.

I guess the Professor was everything I'd imagined he would be – tall, slightly stooping and intensely academic, but not without charm – I guess that's where the cross-dressing came in - when he wasn't adopting his default attitude of grumpy.

'Professor Dawkins, charmed to meet you' he said. 'While I approve of your plans to revolutionise medical care in the sanitorium, I doubt you'll be able to achieve it. This place is lost in history and doesn't take easily to change'.

It could only get better. And don't mention his television appearance as Frank N Furter, I kept telling myself.

He asked me how I had come to be in possession of the data stick.

'How long have you got?' I replied.

He shrugged. 'It was given to me by a desperate man who believed there were dark forces out there who wanted him dead – and sadly, he was right.'

His classroom resembled a mad scientist's laboratory, with test tubes and phials of variously brightly-colored liquids. But Barry looked on in wonder and respect for this man, obviously idolizing him.

'From what I've discovered so far, it doesn't surprise me they wanted him silenced - and you'll be next if you're not careful,' said the Professor. 'Not that I wish to appear melodramatic, but what we have here could destroy the fabric of Western civilization as we know it. If this fell into the wrong hands it could be catastrophic, not only for you and me, but the entire human race. I've been waiting so long for this. Inside this algorithm is the secret of eternal life, something that has been dreamed about since the dawn of man. Up to now, old age has been viewed as a kind of inevitable illness that would kill us all in the end. but not any more, if this formula is correct, which I believe it is. Just imagine the consequences of a small elite using this gift exclusively for their own ends, while denying it to the masses. It would be the greatest inequality ever known to man.'

'And it's nothing to do with the weather, or those female hormones in the sea sending our guys all sissy?' I asked. 'We ladies still need some real men to cater for our needs.'

'So I am led to believe,' he replied. 'And emasculating males could potentially be an excellent form of population control, but we are talking eternal life here.' He was pointing at the PC screen.

'OK, let's get back to emasculation later. So what do you think we should do, Professor?'

'Yes, shall we hand it in to the police?' said Barry, positive and practical as always.

'Most certainly not! Trust no one, except for Doctor Farage,' said the Professor in the gravest of tones. 'Next to me, he is Britain's foremost expert on the search for eternal life, but unlike me, he isn't tainted by scandal, and will be able to keep it out of the hands of those who would use it against us.'

'Let's get cracking,' said Barry, who knew only too well the Professor could be trusted.

'Barry, you need to stay here to concentrate on your studies,' said the Prof. 'But Caroline will be able to find the good doctor in the Derbyshire Peak District, where he lives with his family in a large stone house with a south-facing garden. He will be celebrating his sixtieth birthday tomorrow.'

'Not a good time to call then?' I suggested.

'I will send him an introduction so that he'll be expecting you,' said the Professor. 'I wish you well in your endeavors.' He turned his attention back to an experiment he was conducting regarding dehydration.

At least we now had a plan. I would be leaving first thing, map and Vlad's memory stick in hand. I recalled how on that cursed night he had handed me a map of the Peak District and promised to give me an address before he was so brutally denied the chance. Everything was coming full circle, as prophesied by Vlad. Barry was insisting on travelling with me, but I didn't think he should be missing classes, and anyway this had become something I really needed to do on my own, because only then could I truly move on.

I did ask Barry for his help in faking the annual medical health inspection though, which the Head was so keen for us to oversee.

'The guys are going to be so upset about not getting their once over from you, especially after what happened in the showers,' he said. They don't know the half of it, I wanted to say, although some things are better left unsaid between a group of naked hot guys and an innocent young woman who inadvertently got a little carried away by a bunch of spunky hunks accidentally falling into her little hands. There was going to be no repeat performance.

It didn't take long for Barry to produce an official-looking document detailing the outcome of a full-scale medical examination of the upper sixth which had never happened. He modestly scored himself nine out of ten for his magic wand, while generously awarding three to Winkle for his dinkle.

When Royston heard that the examination had been successfully completed, he was so pleased that he gave me a day's leave and permission to borrow his esteemed Morgan sports car for my drive to the Peak District. What a gracious man he truly was.

CHAPTER THIRTEEN

As Barry kissed me farewell in the stately forecourt of Saint Drongo's School, I could have sworn I saw tears in his eyes. It wasn't as if I was going to be away for very long – it was only a hundred-mile round trip and I would be back within the day – but still he was all teary-eyed at seeing me go.

'Hang on to those pills – and don't tell anybody else about them, not even the Professor,' I cautioned him. He handed me a smartphone which he said was for use in dire emergencies only, as calls could be traced. 'I'll keep it close to my heart,' I teased him, before hitting the accelerator of the Morgan and getting the hell out of there. I do confess to taking particular delight in delivering the caretaker a two-fingered salute as I splashed though a puddle and gave him a long-overdue shower.

I was on the road again and loving it, intoxicated by the freedom of going where the hell I wanted. I called in at a little church in a village called Canwell where I had ancestors buried in the beautifully-kept churchyard there. I followed that by stopping off in the historic city of Lichfield, to dine at a restaurant in the Cathedral Close, in the shadow of the only cathedral with three spires in the whole of the United Kingdom. What a delight to discover the real England at last.

On the last leg of the journey the gentle English countryside gradually transformed into something more rugged and mountainous, with just a hint of a storm brewing under darkening Derbyshire skies. As I continued along the long and winding road, feeling as isolated as a tree stump in a Louisiana swamp, I spied a truck in my rear-view mirror. The driver was clearly monitoring me, as he was hanging back and then accelerating just as I was about to disappear from view. Was I going to end my days gunned down by a sniper on a lonely road in the middle of nowhere?

Then I heard the blast of that distinctive horn, and realized with relief that it was Olaf. As we approached a truckstop he indicated right, and we both turned in.

I was thrilled to see him. 'Olaf, what in the Lord's name are you doing here?' I said as he descended from his cab.

'I'm taking stuff from Poland to England, and then back again. It's what I do,' he replied.

'And there's me thinking you might be keeping an eye on me.'

'As if I would do such a stupid mental thing, you crazy cow,' he said.

'Don't think I don't appreciate it, Olaf. You're like my fairy godmother, keeping me out of harm's way.'

'You like this?'

'Of course I do. I sure could see you in a sparkly dress and a pair of fairy wings. Which might be the way of things, what with all those female hormones in the sea.'

'Not for me, Caro, I ain't no Transylvanian,' he said. We stepped into he café and sat down.

'So, you leave Pearl in Hogwarts to go back to your old man on the boat?' he surmised.

'Not exactly,' I replied as the waiter brought us two mugs of finest English tea and placed them on the rather rickety table for us to drink.

'I'm only going to tell you this 'cos I feel as if I could trust you with my life – so not a word to anybody else.'

'My lips are stitched up,' he promised.

'I'm on a mission to deliver a secret formula to a top expert. That will leave me free to join my one true love, Larry, and to carry on my career where I left off at Capital Talk.'

'So, you'll be back on the radio soon, Miss Caro – brilliant!' he exclaimed.

'You've always been my number one fan, Olaf.'

'And proud of it,' he replied, 'even though I know you could never be my lady. Much too fabulous are you for me, whereas Pearl, maybe she could be my girl?'

'More tea, Olaf? I asked, purely to buy me time to think of ways of letting him down gently. 'I know how fondly Miss Pearl thinks of you, Olaf, but since she's been at that darn school something's happened to her. She's fallen under the under the spell of the headmaster there.'

'What a prostitute!'

'No Olaf – maybe a flibbertigibbet, but no way a prostitute,' I corrected him.

'I will kill that head teacher if he so much as lays a finger on her. She's so pure.'

'I wouldn't be so certain of that. You see Olaf, Miss Pearl is a woman of the world – and I can't help but notice you're wearing a wedding ring too, so I'm guessing there must be a Mrs Olaf back there in Poland.'

'So what if there is? She's a prostitute too. She goes with another man while I'm slaving away on foreign roads, when it should be the other way around.' He put his his big head in his hands. 'Miss Caro, I'm a disgrace to the truck driving community.'

'No, you're not Olaf. In fact it's honest of you to tell me about it.'

'That's another Caro type of thing to say.'

'She probably thinks that a handsome guy like you has been having sexual adventures on the road, and she may only have started cheating 'cos she believes you must be at it too.'

'That could be my wife speaking. You women are all the same, trying to justify your extra sex by referring to noble things, when it's really no different from men's cheating.'

'There's still so much you have to learn about women, Olaf,' I said, pouring him another cup of tea.

'You need to make her feel more secure. Is it any wonder she assumes that a reasonably good-looking guy like you is dating other women while she's stuck back home?'

'You make it seem like it's me who's doing something wrong, Miss Caro.'

' I trust you – and you have to regain your wife's trust too,' I said.

'OK, I try.'

That was the easy part.

'Now listen Olaf, I'm delivering a top-secret theorem to a scientist called Doctor Farage,'

'Oh no, not him! He no like Polskie people, he wants to kick us out of Britain.'

'Not that Farage. This one's a highly reputable scientist who wants to save the world from a disaster which would be a hell of a lot worse than the one the other Farage caused.'

'Whatever you say, Caro, but I go with you anyway, to protect you from all the shit that's flying around.'

What is it with those men in my life, refusing to believe

I could execute even the simplest of tasks, delivering a stick to a scientist? It wasn't rocket science – it was DNA. Not that I didn't appreciate his concern – it's just that sometimes a girl's got to do what a girl's got to do, without some guy screwing it up.

'I promise you, Olaf, once this is all done I'll invite you to our wedding,' I said. That seemed to do little to raise his spirits.

'Not that boat guy. You can do better than that,' he protested.

'Olaf, they don't come much better,' I assured him.

We agreed to meet up again soon, but not before he had tried and failed to persuade me to let me accompany him on my journey to Doctor Farage.

We said our farewells and I climbed back into the Morgan. I was pleased to see that the flags were out en route in the market town of Ashbourne, and a couple of local citizens waved at me, no doubt impressed by Royston's eye-catching car. By the time I got to Dovedale I felt I could seriously begin to look forward to a life without death and danger at every turn, and soon my spirits were higher than a possum eatin' a sweet potato. Not long now and I would be free to resume a more normal life.

I soon found Doctor Farage, who turned out to be a most agreeable man. He welcomed me into his family's home, a handsome house with a grey slate roof.

'Good to meet you, Miss Kennedy. I've heard so

much about you from the Professor,' he said, taking my coat.

'I would have got here sooner but I bumped into a friend along the way,' I explained.

'And is she, or he, still with you?' he asked, looking a touch alarmed at the prospect.

'Oh no – we went our separate ways.'

'Just as well, better that this remains a matter between you and me,' he said. He escorted me into an impressively grand living room with an exceptionally high ceiling, and I was invited to sit down.

'And how is Professor Dawkins? In better spirits, I trust, after that dreadful debacle with him performing the Time Warp on Pointless,' he asked.

'Much improved, and extremely happy teaching at Saint Drongo's. He's real excited but he's deeply concerned about this formula which fell so unexpectedly into my hands,' I said.

'So I'm led to understand,' he said. Just then the door burst open and two teenage girls, pursued by a woman I took to be Mrs Farage, came crashing into the room.

'Come back here this instant!' she shouted. 'You'll have to forgive us, my dear, my daughters are a little excited about going on a foreign holiday at such short notice.'

'How nice, Spain?' I enquired, as if I cared.

'No, a little further east than that,' she replied. 'And please don't take any of this personally, but it's such a shame that a young woman like you should get mixed up in something like this.' She spoke with a real sense of sorrow. As she herded the girls back to their quarters, I wondered what she knew that I didn't.

'Given our imminent departure I'd be most grateful if you could hand over that memory stick, if you please,' Doctor Farage politely requested. Such fine manners – it was a pleasure to be in his company, if only for a short while.

'You're welcome to it,' I said, handing it over as requested. Truly, I hadn't been happier to get rid of anything since losing my virginity. 'Now I can get back to normal life,' I pronounced as I stood up to leave.

'If only that were the case.' He stepped over to the door and locked it. 'The situation is quite the opposite, in fact. I'm afraid this is where it ends for you, Miss Kennedy, or may I call you Caroline? Death is such a personal matter, so it's important we do this in a civilized way.'

'I beg your pardon?' I said, still wanting to keep it polite. What was this guy talking about?

'You could have joined us for lunch had you arrived a little earlier, and then I would have killed you for dessert,' he said. This was getting crazier by the minute.

'Have you taken leave of your senses?' I demanded of him.

'On the contrary, my mind has never been clearer. Although you may feign ignorance of what the memory stick contains, Professor Dawkins advises me that you've already become acquainted with the essence of the algorithm, while cleverly pretending to be stupid. Therefore, I must kill you.'

'Well now, is that the time already?' I said, looking at my watch. 'Much as I'd love to go on chatting to you, I have to get back to Saint Drongo's. The Head wants to discuss what to do about Winkle's exceptionally small winkle,' I said.

'Sit down!' he snapped, gripping me with the force of a madman. It was only then that I noticed that he had a scar under his right eye. *Beware of the man with the scar under his right eye* – that was what poor Vlad had said on that fateful night when I had found him dead in my bed. Suddenly I was beginning to worry.

'You're crazy! They'll all come looking for me, Carla and Pearl, and Inspector Flowers, and Larry of course, not to mention Barry Potter,' I warned him.

'Of course they will, but by that time my family and I will be long gone. Our flight to Moscow leaves Manchester in less than four hours. President Putin's closest aides will be waiting to meet us, so we can assist them in decoding your memory stick and use it for the greater might of Russia.'

'Over my dead body!'

'An apt choice of words indeed,' he said with a mad cackle.

'You really are deluding yourself believing that such

an insane plan could work,' I said, trying to chip away at his self-confidence.

'Oh, it will work. By the time they find your decaying body we will be impossible to reach, and the brilliant Russian doctors will be able to ensure that their glorious leader, Vladimir Putin, will live forever. He will create an eternal dynasty with President Trump on his right hand, ruling the world in tandem, together as one.'

'So that's how Trump managed to win the election. It all makes sense now.'

'Exactly. I can only tell you all this, of course, because you won't be around to see it.'

Personally I always preferred the weather conspiracy, and the female hormones in the sea turning everyone womanly, because without men to screw stuff up none of this insanity would be going on. Hopefully we'd be able to keep a few prize specimens like Larry and Barry in reserve for our womanly delight. I believe the gorillas operate something very similar in central Africa, and it works a treat. But Doctor Farage was in no mood to talk about anything but my impending death, more's the pity.

Maybe if I tried pricking his conscience about loyalty to his country, that might help.

'After everything those superb British universities have given you?' I challenged him.

'I spit on them, with their ridiculously posh voices and their contempt for those like me who come from the wrong side of the tracks. And all those arcane rules and regulations of the British establishment – I'm still not sure how to hold a fork when I go to one of their ridiculous dinners.'

'And that's reason enough to betray your country?'

'It's as good as any, and the hundred million dollars I will receive obviously helps. Also, I believe the Moscow titty bars are of a remarkably high standard. Just a shame you won't be around to make a career in them. You certainly have all the right equipment. Are they natural?'

'Now you're really starting to offend me,' I told him. 'Of course they're real.'

The cheek of the man. That was worse than wanting to kill me.

'Surely you don't want the mess and inconvenience of a body. Couldn't you just tie me up?'

'You'll only go and hand me into the police when you get free. I've told you far too much.'

'We'll just it put it down to a mid-life crisis – you'd be amazed by how many men get them. They come on my show all the time,' I said, still working on him.

'You don't have to suffer. I'll just add a spoonful of this sugar to your tea and you will die quite painlessly within about three minutes.' He offered me the bowl.

'I don't take sugar, it's bad for your health,' I replied.

'Typical American health freak,' he said, and he pulled out a revolver. He lifted the gun and pointed it at my face. Before I could think of any more smart things to say, there was a terrible bang. I felt the most excruciating pain, and everything went blank.

When I came to I was lying on the floor, and there was

still a sharp pain in my chest. I carefully put out a finger, and touched Barry's smartphone, still in my jacket pocket. I drew it out and saw that there was a hole almost clean through it. Well! I've heard of people's lives being saved by their phones by dialing 911, but not quite like this.

I pulled myself up and looked a little closer. There was a nasty bruise, but no blood.

Just then I heard voices in the next room, and realized that getting the hell out of there wouldn't be such a bad idea. But how was I going to get out through a locked door?

Just then there was an almighty crash and the window frame in the front room collapsed inwards, sending splinters of glass flying everywhere.

'Over here, you crazy bitch!' came a shout. Olaf! I ran over to the window and he helped me out through the shattered frame. 'Get the fuck in!' he shouted, pulling me inside and hitting the gas.

'What took you so long?' I asked.

'I wasn't sure you wanted me to help you.'

'I so owe you, Olaf. But first we must get to the nearest police headquarters. We have to stop this crazy doc leaving the country and taking his secrets with him to Russia.'

'Don't you ever switch off? It's like you've become some kind of spy,' said Olaf.

'I guess I have had to learn a few tricks. Thank the Lord you followed me.'

'When I saw you going into that place I decided I ought to have a Plan B,' he explained to me.

'You're a total star. And so's Barry Potter, because his smartphone just stopped a bullet and saved my life.'

'But that Larry of yours, he's done precisely nothing,' said Olaf, rather unfairly I thought.

Thanks to the crazy speed he drove through the Derbyshire Lanes, we were outside Ashbourne Police Station in no time at all.

'Sorry Miss Caro, but you're going to have to go in alone,' Olaf apologetically explained after parking his truck around the corner from the main entrance. 'I don't do police stations. If they check my paperwork they'll have all the excuse they need to get me out the buggering country following Brexit.'

'I'll be fine, you've already done more than enough,' I said, thanking him with a kiss. 'And you need to get back to your wife and start making her feel secure again. Best not tell her about rescuing me though.'

'But I worry big time about you,' said the gallant Olaf.

'I'll be OK. I will demand to speak to Inspector Flowers once Farage has been put under arrest.'

And so he went on his way, and I wondered if I would ever see him again.

The first thing I saw upon entering Ashbourne Police Station was a picture of me, under the heading MOST WANTED. It was on the wall behind the sergeant who was manning the desk. They could have chosen a more flattering photograph.

'My name is Caroline Kennedy and I am here to report an attempt on my life by a certain Doctor Farage,' I solemnly announced. 'I have reason to believe Doctor Farage presents an imminent threat to the security of the United Kingdom, the United States, and the European Union.'

'Name?' was all he had to say.

'I've already told you that, it's Caroline Kennedy, but my listeners know me as Miss Caro. But we're running out of time if we're to keep the secret out of the hands of President Putin and President Trump.'

He didn't look too impressed, as if people popped into Ashbourne Police Station with such tales every day of the week. 'Haven't I seen you somewhere before?' he asked.

'Come on officer, sharpen up.' I pointed to the poster behind him. 'I'm the Killer In High Heels, but before you go arresting me I wish to inform you that I'm completely innocent.'

'They all say that, Miss.'

'I'm the patsy. It's Farage you need to lock up. I'll explain everything to a senior officer.'

I might as well have been speaking in Swahili. 'May I advise you that Doctor Farage is a highly respected local citizen,' replied the officer. 'He's even been on The One Show.'

'That's what he wants you to believe,' I said. 'I demand to speak to the officer in charge.'

'You're talking to him. I'm the only officer here, in fact. It's the cutbacks, you see.'

Just as I was beginning to seriously regret letting Olaf go on his way, who should walk in but Inspector Flowers, to rescue me, I assumed, and still looking hot, accompanied by another cop. And dang me if young Barry wasn't with them too.

'What a relief to see you guys!' I said. 'This is Inspector Flowers, Sergeant. He's been investigating my case for some while now. And this is Barry Potter, the boy wonder from Saint Drongo's. Am I pleased to see you two.'

'Me too,' said the sergeant, 'left alone in the station with a cold-blooded killer like her.'

'You can relax now, Sergeant Rudd. I don't think Miss Kennedy will be posing a threat to you, or anybody else, for a very long time,' he said weirdly, like I was guilty or something. Barry was wearing an uncharacteristic fixed grin.

'What's wrong with you guys?' I asked them. 'You don't seem to know whether to check your ass or scratch your watch.'

'Don't make this difficult for yourself, Miss Kennedy,' said Inspector Flowers, addressing me like I was just another criminal, instead of somebody whose bed he'd slept in, even if it was top to toe.

'OK, so maybe it doesn't look that good, having spent so long before getting in touch, but what with everything being so darn complicated, and being hijacked by this teenage boy, I didn't know whether I was coming or going. Oh Lordy, I should have listened to Larry and given myself up, straight away.'

'At least it will help you in mitigation that you eventually decided to hand yourself in,' the Inspector said. Barry unaccountably nodded in agreement.

'So, what's with you, Barry Potter?' I couldn't help but berate him. 'I thought you were supposed to be on my side, looking at me with your puppy dog eyes, and wanting to get all jiggy with me, when all along you were part of this conspiracy to get me framed – and there's no other word for it.'

'It's not like that, Miss Caro,' Barry pleaded.

'Only my friends call me Miss Caro, and you'll never be my friend again,' I said.

'The good Professor has been like a father to me at school. What was I supposed to believe when he took me into his confidence and explained how he'd seen through your plan to pretend to be ignorant? Of course I argued against it, until he persuaded me that you were in league with a hostile foreign power.'

'Then the Professor has got it badly wrong. Or maybe he's been in league with Farage since the beginning – that must be it. Look, Farage tried to shoot me, and your phone stopped the goddam bullet!' I waved the evidence at them. But they didn't want to know.

I could see how much this was hurting Barry, although

not as much as it was hurting me. Sergeant Rudd was still singing Farage's praises as a fine local upstanding citizen who gave generously to the Police Benevolent Fund. I bet he bloody did.

'I demand that you call Doctor Farage and put all my allegations to him,' I said to the Sergeant. I was clutching at straws now, having lost the support of Barry and Flowers. It was almost certainly going to be a complete waste of time, but what else could I do?

But the Sergeant agreed to call him, and put it on speakerphone so we could all hear.

'Good evening, Doctor. We've got a lady here who is claiming you tried to harm her person,' said the Sergeant in his tortuous English.

'That's utterly preposterous. It couldn't be further from the truth,' we heard him say.

'So, you admit to knowing the young lady in question?' said the Sergeant, promisingly.

'Assuming it's the same woman, she made an uninvited call to our home – my wife and two daughters also met her – but she refused to leave without being given a large amount of money, and threatened to make unfounded allegations against me unless I paid up.'

'There's a word for people like that, sir,' said the Sergeant.

'Yes. And of course I had no idea she was a deranged murderer, until I caught up with the television news just a few minutes ago.'

'I'm most grateful sir. I won't be bothering you again,'

he said, and placed the phone back on its perch.

We all waited for the inevitable next step, being familiar with TV cop shows through the decades. Inspector Flowers prepared to do his worst.

'Caroline Kennedy, I'm arresting you on suspicion of the murder of Vlad Kaspersky. You do not have to talk, I mean speak, but it may ruin your case if you do not mention questions which you later on use in court.'

'In other words, you're nicked,' said the Sergeant. Inspector Flowers locked one end of a pair of handcuffs on to my wrist, and it hurt.

'Is that strictly necessary?' said Barry.

'No point in getting all concerned now, young Barry,' I said.

It was as if Barry Potter had suddenly lost his invincibility cloak and had become mortal like the rest of us poor suckers. He certainly looked taken aback when he was told he wasn't yet free to go, and would be travelling with us to police HQ in Derbyshire for further verification, whatever that might mean. Flowers then handcuffed Barry to me to ensure what he described as our mutual safety. That got the boy's heart thumping, and his mind racing too, by the look of him. He wasn't expecting that.

'Nice work, Barry Potter. And I used to think you were so freaking clever,' I said as we were directed to the back seat of their unmarked car.

'It doesn't make any difference to the way I feel about

you,' said Barry, quite incredibly. 'I'll wait for you, and I'll be there for you when you've served your sentence. I'll be quite a lot older by then, which might suit you better.'

'But surely I'll be too old for you by then? It could be decades. Somehow I don't think you'll be there to greet me the day I'm set free.'

'You can count on me Miss Caro, I'll be there for you, however long it takes, because I love you, you crazy lady.'

'Well, you've got a darn funny way of showing it,' I said as Flowers got in the driver's seat and accelerated away.

CHAPTER FOURTEEN

You have to admit that considering Barry now believed I was the most evil woman on Planet Earth, the fact that he still wanted me to be his girl was pretty darn romantic. I sp'ose you could call it real love – not a simple rush of the blood to the head, or anywhere else for that matter. But just look where love had got us – handcuffed together in the back of an unmarked police car which was heading to heaven knows where.

Flowers was driving around those sharp mountainous bends like a bobcat after a chipmunk. If he misjudged one, I figured death was inevitable.

'Any chance we could go a little slower?' I asked.

'And that's the third turning you've missed to

Buxton. In fact, you seem to be going in totally the wrong direction,' Barry advised.

'Just leave it to us, young sir,' said Flowers, and I gave Barry one of my withering stares. 'So, you haven't figured it out yet, young Potter? These guys are no more cops than I'm the Killer In High Heels.'

'Show me your evidence,' he challenged me.

'There are more clues than you get in a book of crosswords. How could I have fallen for Flowers? And to think I allowed him to sleep in my home. When he read me the caution back there at the police station he was all over the shop. There were so many mistakes that even an American like me couldn't help but notice, being a fan of the late lamented Inspector Morse. Then handcuffing us together, and not releasing you – none of it adds up, Barry.'

That gave Barry something to think about. I felt utterly betrayed by the dashing Inspector Flowers, who was no more a policeman than I was a Russian spy. And to think he'd stayed overnight in my home, just the two of us – it's a wonder I hadn't been murdered in my bed.

Even Flowers was now forced to drive more cautiously because a heavy mist had now fallen upon us, making it hard for him to see beyond the end of his nose.

Suddenly a flock of sheep appeared from nowhere and he was forced to slam on his brakes, much to the annoyance of our short-tempered jailers.

'I need to use the bathroom,' I told them.

'She's trying it on,' said the accomplice.

'She won't get far in this weather, not with the boy attached to her,' said Flowers.

'Anytime soon,' I urged them.

'Don't get wandering too far away, Miss,' said Flowers.

'Only as far as modesty requires,' I replied, all prim and proper.

'And keep an eye on her, Mr Potter – you'll be our eyes and ears out there.'

Flowers checked my handbag, and embarrassingly found my Rampant Rabbit. Well, it had been a fair few days since I'd seen Larry, not that I was going to apologize for it.

'I trust that doesn't make you feel too inadequate, Inspector,' I said contemptuously.

We didn't have to walk far before Barry and I found a suitably secluded spot, and as luck would have it, the mist was thicker here.

'Shall I look the other way?' Barry asked.

'No, we're gonna run for our lives, 'cos these guys are going to kill us both, Barry.'

I still wasn't sure he'd really got it, but just in case he needed any further persuasion I pulled out my vibrator and poked it hard into his back, the way a real killer in high heels would do if she was armed with a gun instead of one of Ann Summers' finest.

'Be afraid Barry, be very afraid, 'cos when you've already killed once, what difference does it make if you kill again?' I pressed the Rampant Rabbit into the small of his back. 'Now when I say go, I want you to run like the wind, and follow me, through streams, up hills and down dales. Now go!'

He didn't argue, and we took flight through frosty fields full of bleating sheep, running ever further into the thickening gloom. 'You'll never survive the night out there,' I heard Flowers shout as he realized we had made a run for it. For a while I could hear our captors' voices in the distance but they soon faded to silence.

I might as well die from exposure on a Derbyshire hillside as from a bullet in some random cellar somewhere. And to think, I once had feelings for that guy.

But then I heard their voices getting closer again. How the hell did that happen? We must have gone round in a circle. Sure enough, we had come to a bridge, and were back on the road again.

'Come back here or we'll start firing live rounds!' I heard his accomplice shout. 'This way,' I ordered Barry, dragging him down a perilously steep embankment. We hid under a bridge standing knee-deep in a freezing cold stream, him with a sex aid in his back.

Mercifully, they didn't hang around too long and the sound of their voices disappeared into the distance again. They were mumbling oaths and curses, telling each other they would both be for it. Meanwhile we trudged across the moors, getting colder and ever more desperate as each hour went by.

'I had my whole life ahead of me,' said Barry, feeling sorry for himself.

'And I didn't? I'm not that much older than you,' I replied.

'At last she finally admits it, on a freezing moor when we're about to die from exposure. How appropriate. And it's my birthday tomorrow.'

At last we came to a deserted road. Perhaps this would get us back on track.

'If a Polish truck comes this way, flag it down. Otherwise hide behind the levee,' I instructed Barry. But we didn't need to do either of those things, because then I saw a shape through the gloom, and the most unlikely vision materialized – a place of bright lights, the sound of laughter and Ed Sheeran songs, with a sign that said 'Four Winds Public House and Hotel'.

'I do declare, Barry Potter, I think we've only gone and found ourselves a pub!' I cried. While I've often heard folks saying they were dying for a drink, for once it looked like a pub had really saved our lives. And it looked like they had rooms, because there was a most welcome sign reading 'Accommodation Available' above the front door.

'Salvation is at hand, Barry Potter, but I don't want you giving us away, or our days will be numbered,' I reminded him, delivering a short sharp stab in the back with my vibrator, just to concentrate his mind.

We pushed open the door to be greeted by the warm

glow of a traditional log fire and a cheery welcome from a rosy-cheeked landlord who'd been busy chatting to his customers at the bar.

'Stay close,' I mouthed at Barry Potter, as if he had any choice in the matter, handcuffed as he was to the Killer In High Heels. 'And do what I tell you,' I said, giving him another serious prod in the back. Some men I've known would pay good money for that.

'What brings you two love birds out on a night like this?' asked the landlord.

'Our car broke down about a mile and a half down the road, so we walked the rest of the way here,' I explained in my finest West Midland accent.

'Reckon you could both be doing with one of these,' he said, pouring us a couple of glasses of whisky with a dash of hot water and herbs in each.

'Aw, that's bostin," I said, gratefully knocking mine back. Barry sipped his more cautiously.

'You could have frozen to death out there. Why didn't you phone for help?' the landlord asked me.

'I couldn't get a signal.'

'Ah, Vodafone.'

'Vodafone… yep, that's right.'

'Their users always struggle to get a signal round here,' he explained. He tried his whisky and immediately choked on it. It suddenly dawned upon me that he wasn't even legally permitted to consume booze in this guy's pub.

'Not a lover of strong spirits, are we sir?' said the landlord.

'I couldn't help but notice that you provide accommodation,' I said to him, trying to change the subject. I didn't want him asking to see Barry's ID.

'Yes, we most certainly do, and you're in luck. We had a late cancellation from a honeymoon couple, only because of the weather you understand, so you'd be most welcome to stay in our bridal suite.'

'How nice,' I said through gritted teeth. Barry suddenly perked up, becoming much more like his old self.

'And who would like to sign the register?'

'That would be me,' I said without hesitation.

'In my day, it was the fellas who had to do all the official stuff, but now anything goes,' he said. Opposite 'NAME' I put down the first thing that came into my head, the name of a brand of port which caught my eye on the shelf above the bar.

'That all appears to be above board, Mr and Mrs Cock-burn,' he said. Barry coughed on his drink again.

'It's actually pronounced Coburn, without the K – you should know that, landlord, being a purveyor of the stuff.'

'Forgive me, but we don't get too much call for port round these parts.'

Just then a woman who I presumed to be his wife emerged from the lounge bar to give us the once over, no doubt wondering about our bedraggled appearance. As soon as she was satisfied by our explanation, she reprimanded her husband for failing to provide us with night clothes and basic toiletries. 'Honestly Mick, what could you have been thinking of, treating our young guests like that?' she apologized unnecessarily.

Of course, we had to stay close, and we held our hands together in Barry's pocket to hide those handcuffs from public view. They must have thought we were inseparable – which we were, of course. She doted on us after that, clucking like a mother hen all the way to our suite, where she promised to return later with some hot drinks and two plates of fish and chips, and left us to ponder on how to manage that darn four poster bed.

'If it wasn't for these wretched handcuffs you'd be sleeping on the sofa, Barry Potter,' I reminded him.

'OK, if that's what you want to believe,' he replied.

'And just in case you've got any thoughts about trying to escape while I'm sleeping and revealing the whereabouts of the Killer In High Heels, just remember, I've got a gun under my pillow, loaded and ready to blow you away.' That wiped the smile from his face.

When Hilda, the landlord's wife. delivered a nightdress for me and PJs for Barry, I sensibly suggested that we should divest ourselves of our wet clothes and slip into our sleeping attire, but that was easier said than done, considering we were locked together.

'First, let's take off those pants,' I suggested. That

made him lively again, until I reminded him that 'pants' is American for trousers. I unbuckled his belt and opened his zipper, then we slid our wrists in tandem up and down his muscular legs to get his pants off. Not an unpleasant way of passing an evening, I have to admit. I had not really expected Barry to be hairy, but his legs certainly were, although he had a remarkably smooth back and even smoother bum cheeks, which I happened to catch sight of when he removed his Calvin Kleins. I had promised to keep my eyes shut but I couldn't resist a swift glimpse – well, it would have been weird not to. And then we got him into his PJ trousers, and it was just as well they were baggy, given the amount of uprising in those frontal regions, which I tried my hardest to ignore.

'I'm eighteen tomorrow, and here I am still being dressed by an adult,' he said.

'Make the most of it Barry, you never know when it's going to come your way again,' I replied.

We carried on with our game of getting undressed while manacled together, and I invited Barry to unclip my bra while I went into an arm lock. We moved our wrists up and down my legs to remove my damp tights, and then somehow I slipped into the landlady's spare baby doll nightie. It was all far too much fun considering the boy had got us into this darn fix in the first place.

Fortunately just then Hilda herself came knocking on our door again, to let us know that she'd left a tray of food and drinks the other side of the door, and not to let it go cold.

'I'm starving,' said Barry.

'Me too,' I said. We shuffled our way to the tray and proceeded to feed one another as best we could. As soon as we had finished eating we headed towards the four-poster bed, where it didn't take long for us both to drop off, sleeping fitfully and uncomfortably as the night progressed. Once or twice I was woken up by my arm being yanked across by Barry as he turned in his sleep, and at other times I felt a familiar prodding in my back from him, although this time it most definitely wasn't a gun.

'I'll give you five minutes to stop doing that, Barry Potter,' I warned him, but I didn't stay awake to see it out, so tired was I. I fell into a much deeper sleep – until I awoke to discover that something was missing from the end of my arm, and its name was Barry Potter. He must have somehow freed himself from the handcuffs. My first reaction was that I'd lost him for good, and in spite of his love for me I'd also witnessed how much he respected the law. He had probably called the police even as I lay there in our marital bed. Just as long as it wasn't that fake Inspector Flowers who was going to come running to take me back into custody.

But when the knock eventually came, in walked Barry with a warm but penitent smile upon his face. He was carrying a tray piled high with cereal and bacon and eggs, and a flask full of coffee. Suddenly he looked adorable in his striped pajamas.

'Breakfast for Madam,' he announced in the style of one of the hot male servants from Downton Abbey.

'Well dang me. I thought I'd lost you, Barry Potter. I never believed you'd come back to me,' I confessed.

'As if you could think such a thing! I'd already decided not to desert you again, whether you were guilty or not. Although I never really believed you killed Vlad, unless it was from sexual exhaustion.' He grinned and sat me up in bed, putting a pillow behind my back and then placing the tray on the bed for me.

'How did you get out of the handcuffs?' I asked.

'It's amazing what you can do with a large tub of Vaseline and a high pain threshold,' he replied.

'Funny, that's exactly what Miss Pearl said to me the other day,' I remarked.

'And having got free I went straight to your handbag to get hold of your gun, only to discover that it was something else entirely.'

'A woman has needs, Barry.'

'Not when I'm around, Miss Caro,' he cheekily replied.

Trouble was, he may well have been right, judging by all that night-time prodding.

'So having discovered that I'd allowed myself to be threatened by a vibrator...'

'Many men are.'

'...I thought I would nip downstairs for a nightcap, but when I got out on to the landing, who should be leaning against the bar but Flowers and his accomplice, chatting away to Mick the landlord. Then while he was away changing a barrel in the cellar, the hoodlums began discussing everything that had been going on. Apparently, Farage and his family were detained soon after touching down in Moscow, and the memory stick contained nothing more earth-shattering than a classic scene from a Muppet Christmas Carol – not what the Russians were expecting at all.'

'How in God's green earth did that happen?,' I asked him, tucking into the cooked breakfast.

'I took the precaution of adding a virus to make the data turn into scenes from legendary children's movies after a matter of hours. I did the same with all the copies.'

'I just knew you'd come good again, Barry.'

'But not quite good enough. They've been able to get one of the sticks to Mr Know All the Human Search Engine, an old-style music hall act who operates out of The Hackney Empire.'

'I know him well,' I said.

'They paid him to learn it as back up if the formula was corrupted by the likes of me. And here's the really weird bit, they're all meeting at the Hackney Empire tonight to smuggle the memory man out of the country, once he's finished his spot on tonight's show.'

'He was top of the bill the night I met Vlad,' I said.

'So I've booked us tickets for tonight's performance.'

'I would expect nothing less of you.'

'Then when the landlord returned from the cellars the hoodlums started to ask him some searching questions about who was staying in the hotel overnight. Just as he was about to spill the beans along came Hilda to the rescue, giving them all grief – to Mick about illegally serving drinks out of hours, and how it could lead to the closure of the pub – and to Flowers and his goon about trying it on, shooing them out of the door, and locking it behind them.'

'She just saved our lives, Barry.'

'And maybe the planet too. So Hilda gave Mike another dressing down, accusing him of being about to give us away. 'Can't you see they're runaways?' she scolded him, 'an older woman and a younger man, no doubt disapproved of by their friends and families, and those guys were detectives, trying to track them down. 'How could you possibly know that?' asked Mick. 'Female intuition,' Hilda replied. Didn't you notice, your old fool, they're so much in love they couldn't bear to be more than a couple of feet apart?

'After that I went back to our bedroom and got on the couch to grab a few hours' sleep, but not before I'd tucked you in and moved the hair from your eyes.'

'I guess I ought to be grateful to you, Barry Potter,' I said. I was getting fond of him all over again.

'But I'll never forgive myself for turning you in,' he confessed.

'Men always let me down. Why should you be any different?'

'If it had been anyone else but the Professor doubting your credibility I'd have never have fallen for it. You see, he's always been there for me in the absence of a father. How could he have deceived me?'

I left Barry to go ponder for a while while I took a shower. I luxuriated under the streams of hot water trickling down my breasts, soaping them sensuously, until I realised someone was taking a sneaky glimpse through the glass. I guess adolescent boys can't really help themselves.

'I'll give you ten minutes to stop looking, Barry,' I said, but once he realized he'd been rumbled he took flight. I kind of liked that he was still boyish enough to fear being caught out for doing something naughty, and not the world-weary gigolo of Leamington Spa Guest House infamy.

I considered how he'd continued to love me, unaffected by his mistaken belief that I may have murdered a man and was preparing to betray the Western world. How could I not forgive him for handing me in? He was only doing what he thought was the right thing for Queen and Country. But why should I worry anyway? Larry was my man. He was a real grown-up manly man, the type I needed, as a real grown-up womanly woman with needs and desires.

And yet I couldn't get young Barry out of my mind, imagining us showering together, him caressing my body, soaping one another down. That was enough of that, I thought as I drenched myself in Chanel Number Five and then slipped into another of Hilda's surprisingly sexy baby doll night dresses, probably left behind by some horny bride on her wedding night. And why not a slash of red lipstick to show passion, plus some dark eye shadow and fake eye lashes to complete the look? This wasn't for Barry or Larry, but for me, because this was who I was, regardless of them.

It was then that I was interrupted by my phone bleeping. It displayed a text from a number I didn't recognize. I was horrified to see that it was from Larry's wife. How the hell did she get my number? My reflex reaction was to press delete, but then I thought better of it. I just had to read what she'd sent me, however much I hated it. Maybe she was glad to be letting him go.

I bet you believe you're so special now you're the one – or at least you think you are, 'cos don't delude yourself honey when he says he's leaving me for you. He's done this so many times before with a string of young naive girls, so welcome to the club of poor deceived women he's run off until he eventually comes home to me. But I'm not having him back this time – you're welcome to him, he's all yours, that is until he tires of you and the next one comes along, younger and prettier than you. Then you'll know how it feels. I hope he hurts you nearly as much as he hurt me. Do you know what? He even got down on one knee and proposed marriage to some of these poor girls – maybe he's already done that to you, so I wouldn't order your wedding dress just yet.

Well at least he'd kept his part of the bargain and told her he was leaving. But this was one bitter middle-aged woman, which was only to be expected. And who could blame her for wanting to blacken Larry's name by saying he'd done it before? They were surely just an invention intended to hurt me. Larry wasn't cheating on me but on her, and it was driving her to distraction and sending her loopy enough to make stuff up.

But what if she was telling the truth? Perhaps he had led me a merry dance, and there really were others he'd played the same game with. Suddenly it began to have the ring of truth about it, and the feeling of being betrayed overwhelmed me. I couldn't go on living in denial any longer if I was just another notch on Larry's love boat. Well, if that was true, nobody puts Miss Caro in the cargo hold.

I looked at myself in the mirror and knew exactly what had to be done, and who it had to be done with. His name was Barry Potter, and he had now turned 18.

I sashayed back into our bedroom, telling him I had a very special present for him, and proceeded to perform 'Happy Birthday To You' in the style of Marilyn Monroe to JFK. He watched open-mouthed.

'That's my best birthday present ever,' he said.

'Well that was just for starters,' I whispered into his ear.

Maybe you don't need to know what happened next, about how he made me feel more like a natural-born woman than anyone else ever had before or since. Boy had those bitch friends of his mom's taught him well, with that unique mix of endearing sweetness and full-on fucking force. 'And I used to think you were just a boy,' I said.

I sure didn't expect him to exceed my wildest fantasy. His foreplay made me go swimmy-headed with sheer delight, every fibre of my being brought to a climax that could have gone thermo-nucleur at any moment.

Sure he was built for the job, but it was what he did with that thing which got me gagging for more. Electric charges of joy were pulsating all over me. And then came the moment I had truly been waiting for when he entered me. He went thrillingly deep down, ocean deep inside me, and that sensation transcended every song I'd ever heard, every dance I had ever seen and every man I'd ever encountered, for this was a paranormal wand which befitted his magical name, and he knew exactly how to cast its spell all over me.

And having entered me, on and on and on and on it went, the never-ending cock and bringer of consummate joy. How far could it go, and how much bigger could it grow? To fucking infinity and beyond, like some kind of Sex Toy Story, except that this was real. The boy had truly become a man, and I never once felt that I was taking advantage of him, as he was always in control of me, which was just how I liked it – submissive in the bedroom but in control everywhere else.

But when he encouraged me to go on top of him in our love-making I enjoyed the best fucking bucking bronco of my life.

Ride him cowgirl! I shouted out loud, waving my imaginary hat in the air.

And if that wasn't great enough, then he ravished me from behind, his hands on my tits while he pumped me full of his love juice and I climaxed like a yodeling farm girl who'd abandoned her herd for an almighty roll in the hay with the most macho cow poke ever to wander into town.

Of course, It's easy to forget just how much spunk an eighteen-year young man in his prime is capable of splashing out. It gets everywhere, and his tasted as sweet as honey. I licked it off him with the tip of my tongue, then placed my head on his masculine chest, safe in the adorably strong arms of this astonishing pleaser of women.

But I don't want to objectify him any more. In truth, everything Barry Potter did was magic, although if I hadn't received that text from Larry's wife, maybe I would never have found out.

CHAPTER FIFTEEN

Having been well and truly ravished, I now had a world to save, as Barry reminded me. There was no time to discuss what this morning's ravishing meant for our realtionship. I rather suspect that Barry had assumed that by getting jiggy together we were now as good as betrothed, but I was just blissfully confused, unsure whether I should be with Barry or Larry. I was torn between two great lovers, and with an evil plot to foil.

And then my phone rang. I braced myself for the voice of Larry's wife, only to hear Larry instead. 'Caro, it's me,' he said.

I'm not quite sure what he was expecting, perhaps for me to sing Rule Britannia while waving my brassiere around my head.

'Is it?' was all I managed as a reply.

'What the hell have you been doing? I thought when we said goodbye at Moor Street Station you were on your way to hand yourself into Inspector Flowers.'

'Just as well I didn't. He's a fraud, like certain other men I know.'

'Have you been speaking to my wife?'

'No,' I replied.

'That's a relief.'

'But I've been reading a text from her, all about the other girls you've run away with until you were ready to go back home, just like you did with me all those years ago.'

There followed a long silence – a sure sign of guilt if ever there was one.

'I know it doesn't look good Caro, but you mustn't believe a word she says,' he finally replied. 'You see, she's become so bitter and twisted that she'd do anything to destroy my future once I told her that I was leaving her for you.'

'I guess,' I said. Admittedly I had wondered if she was simply out for revenge.

'There's only ever been you, Caro. Of course, I looked at other girls since you and I finished – that's what happens when a guy gets trapped in a loveless marriage – but never, ever have I cheated on you.'

I have to admit he did sound believable. I was once

again reminded that one of the many reasons I'd loved him was because he was the most honest and trustworthy guy I'd ever met. It seemed like I'd conveniently forgotten that fact while I was with Barry. Fortunately, Barry was downstairs for the moment sorting out the bill.

'You've got to believe me, Caro,' he begged . 'Please tell me you understand?'

It would have been hard not to. I realized I would at least have to give him the benefit of the doubt until we could talk face to face. After all, we'd claimed one another as the love of our lives, so I owed him that much, and my feelings for him hadn't been washed away by one night's passion with Barry, although it was a close-run thing.

'I understand,' I replied.

'Oh, thank God.'

'I'll meet you at the Hackney Empire Theatre in London tonight,' I said.

'Whatever for?' he replied.

'I've got a little business to attend to there, which involves clearing my name and preventing Armageddon.'

'I'll be there for you,' he said.

Then we had that thing of who was going to finish the call first, as if nothing had ever happened between Barry and me. Finally hung up first after my fourth attempt to say the last goodbye.

But then Barry came back after paying the bill, full of the joys of spring after having sex with his dream girl, and immediately I felt I'd been unfaithful to him just by talking to Larry.

'Caro, we need to talk about last night,' said Barry.

Truly, that was the last thing I needed. 'It was totally lovely Barry, but we need to get going saving the world, and all that jazz,' I replied.

Just when I thought I was back in love with Larry, Barry only goes and says something really beautiful. 'Not sure if I care about the world any more, Miss Caro, if you and I aren't in it together,' he replied.

'Kiss me, Barry Potter,' I instructed him, and he obeyed. It would most certainly have led to more, but just then I heard the roar of a ten-wheeler truck outside.

'Oh Lordy, it's Olaf! There goes your blow job, Barry,' I said reluctantly. Not that I wasn't pleased to see Olaf, and we needed to get to the Hackney Empire from the middle of nowhere pretty darn quick, so a truck would do nicely. We gave Mick and Hilda a fond farewell, thanking them profusely for keeping our secret and promising them (at their request) an invitation to our wedding, because doubts about Barry and me were multiplying following that phone call with Larry.

'Let's do this Olaf,' I said. His truck couldn't have been less suited for those narrow mountain roads, but it didn't take too long before we were driving on a highway and descending to sea level, where I felt more confident in updating him about what had been going on.

'We're off to the theatre,' I explained. I began to acquaint him with the latest leg of our adventure, including how Inspector Flowers wasn't quite all he seemed and we had managed to escape from him on a cold Derbyshire Moor, before being saved by a pub in the night.

'Can I come to the show too?' he not unreasonably asked.

'Why ever not? You're one of the gang Olaf. In fact, let's make it a group outing. I'm going to invite my friend, boss and confidante, Carla. I'm in need of some level-headed advice.'

'And Miss Pearl too,' said Olaf, obviously still smitten by her.

'Then we mustn't forget her gentleman friend, Royston, my Headmaster,' Barry suggested, although Olaf appeared less enthused by that prospect.

I couldn't wait to see everybody, although it would be a gathering from hell, considering all the unresolved issues which existed between so many of them.

Once we hit the motorway we began to eat up the miles, and that divine sense that London was getting nearer became apparent. How I loved that city, and how I had missed it. It had got under my skin and into my heart all over again. We weren't sure whether we should call in at our house in Hampstead though, as it could well have been under surveillance both by the cops and enemies of the State, or at least so Barry believed. Unfortunately I needed a change of outfit and access to my much-missed wardrobe of designer and vintage clothes, and no dumb conspiracy theory was going to rob me of looking good on our big night.

'It's called getting your priorities right,' I explained to Barry. That boy still had so much to learn.

What bliss it was to emerge from my own shower to have a choice of clothes to wear, putting on various outfits then wearing the first one I'd tried – every woman's birthright. Plus, I'd forgotten just how many shoes I had to choose from. Maybe I wasn't cut out to live on a canal barge after all – one of the many subjects I would have to speak to Larry about. He really needed to understand what sort of person I'd become in the last few weeks and learn to deal with it.

Then we needed to talk about those girls who'd been supposedly hanging out on his boat. I wouldn't be mentioning Barry Potter though – that was simply an honest mistake, although it most certainly didn't feel like it at the time.

After everything that had gone down I couldn't wait to see Larry in the flesh again and be reminded of why he was still the one. In fact, we would all be meeting at the Old Ship Inn, like a get together for some dysfunctional family. The first to arrive was Carla, who greeted me with a mixture of warmth and disbelief.

'I said to go fix your love life, not disappear for six weeks after murdering some guy you picked up at a party,' she mock-reprimanded me.

'If only it was that simple,' I replied, and we both dissolved into laughter.

'I'm loving the red wig,' she observed.

'It's a long story.'

'Look, now I can see you're OK I want you back on air just as soon as you've sorted yourself out,' she said. 'The listeners have been missing you – and no going to the papers, because I demand the exclusive rights, after everything you've put me through.'

'You've got it. With a little luck everything should be resolved this evening and then we'll all be able to move on,' I said, like the cock-eyed optimist I so clearly was.

'At an old-style variety show – how's that going to happen?' she not unreasonably asked.

'It just will, because we've got Barry Potter, and he has this uncanny knack of making good stuff happen,' I said. I pointed him out to her – he was buying a round of drinks at the bar.

'He looks like a fine young man, Caro. Is he your new beau?' she asked me.

'Absolutely not!' I replied a little too forcefully. 'He's just a geeky kid who tagged along, 'cos what he doesn't know about algorithms and formulas and memory sticks ain't worth knowing, and it's come in kind of handy as I seem to have got myself mixed up in a conspiracy which has gone way over my head.'

'I never thought I'd hear Caro uttering the dreaded word 'conspiracy' like she meant it,' said Carla.

'Well, make the most of it, because it sure ain't going to happen again,' I warned her, just in case she was expecting me to change my tune when I returned to the radio.

'So, Larry still measured up?'

Not as well as Barry, I wanted to reply. 'It was as if we had never been apart,' I said instead, explaining that he would be joining us any moment soon, so she could make her own mind up.

'I can't wait to meet him, but I do like the look of that Barry Potter – he's the sort of man who could turn a gay girl straight.'

'But he's only just turned 18,' I said.

'That's legal, isn't it? And he has the confidence of a guy in his thirties. You're losing your touch, Caro – you'd have snapped him up in our West Country days.'

'Exactly. That's why I'm different now, 'cos I've got Larry, and I don't need to bother with the likes of him anymore.'

'And who's that retro-guy getting all lovey-dovey with London's number one transgender DJ, Pearl The Girl?'

'That's Royston, the esteemed headmaster of Saint Drongo's Boarding School. He's been so kind and helpful to me, and he's become devoted to Miss Pearl. I reckon she likes the idea of becoming a headmaster's respectable wife, all twin sets and pearls, and he's more than receptive to the idea.'

'She'll still have to do her show at the weekend –

maybe live from the school dormitory,' she said, still as controlling as ever.

And then to complete my dysfunctional family, in walked Larry, looking almost as adorable as when I'd last seen him. We kissed each other as passionately as being in a public place would allow, although I do wish Barry hadn't seen it.

'Carla, meet Larry,' I said.

'I hear you intend to make an honest woman of her at long last,' said Carla.

'I do,' he replied.

'Oh, I'm so pleased. I'm not sure I could have endured another year of 'will he ever leave his wife'.'

'I'm sorry that my marriage of over twenty years has proved to be such an irritation to you,' he replied.

Ouch! I so needed them to get on together.

'Carla didn't mean any harm darling,' I told him. 'And you're so going to love talking to one another about canal restoration, and radio ratings, and your kids, and how Carla finally came out...'

And then the penny finally dropped. They had nothing in common with one another whatsoever.

'OK, so this, darling, is Pearl,' I said, imagining he would be more at home with a traditional girl. 'But you probably remember her as Stan the Man, my ex-fiancé, when you and I lived next door to one another in Wolverhampton.'

'Give me strength! You're that idiot who used be on

the radio, the chap who couldn't satisfy his wife to be,' he said.

'That's one way of putting it,' Pearl graciously replied, 'although I'm now the person I was truly meant to be.'

'Which is?' he asked.

'A woman, obviously,' she replied, sounding as proud as a sow who'd just given birth.

'Who was born a man? How does that work – just putting on a frock and a bit of make-up doesn't make you female.'

I feared Royston might be about to thump Larry, and I wouldn't have blamed him. I put Larry's rather unfortunate foray into my social circle down to him being a country boy born and bred who had an almost allergic reaction to our fancy London ways. Maybe he was feeling threatened. Anyway I decided not to ask Carla what she thought of him quite yet. And then in walked Olaf, having just parked his truck.

'Hello you fuckers!' he cried out.

'Olaf, language please!' I said.

'So sorry Miss Caro, only trying to be like a friendly kind of Polskie guy,' he replied. Larry looked on in bewilderment.

'Who's been teaching him English? Danny Dyer?' Carla enquired.

OK, so Olaf's grasp of English wasn't exactly perfect, but it was a darn sight better than all our Polish put together. However, this was fast turning into the family reunion from hell, not exactly helped by Barry sitting down opposite us, and glaring menacingly at Larry. I guessed a threesome would be out the question - pity. It was a blessing to make our way to the theatre where they just had to sit back, shut up and watch the show. Only trouble was the plain-clothes cops patrolling the foyer and putting me on edge.

'Am I about to get arrested?' I asked Barry, still my go-to guy, regardless of Larry now being around.

'Not yet, they're using you as bait. They're tracking down your every move in the hope that you'll lead them to Mr Big.'

'Stop filling her head with all this conspiracy nonsense,' said Larry, interrupting our conversation. Maybe he was just a teeny bit jealous – and now that I had experienced Barry's forbidden fruits, he had reason to be.

'Butt out, grandad, we're trying to save the world here,' said Barry.

'Boys, boys!' I interjected before it all got of hand,

'Look, there's Farage in the muppet box,' said Barry, pointing. He was seated overlooking the auditorium, alongside his wife, and much to Barry's distress, Professor Dawkins, who was clearly in on the plot.

'Stop whispering, you two,' said Larry. He was really starting to get on my nerves.

'I'll have you know Larry, that man up there attempted to shoot me dead, and it was only Barry's phone next to my heart that saved me from being his latest victim.'

'When you put it like that,' said Larry, smiling. Well, he was a kind and generous man.

'I thought Farage had been sent to Siberia?' I enquired of Barry as the lights dimmed.

'The Russians must have given him a second chance to get the algorithm back to Moscow, and Mr Know All is his way of achieving it.'

'Milk Cluster?' Larry asked, having thoughtfully purchased a box of chocolates prior to the performance.

'You're OK,' I said. I had lost my appetite upon seeing the fake inspector Flowers entering the muppet box, hovering menacingly between Farage and Dawkins. To think he once used to make my heart race faster than an Atlanta-bound express train.

The lights dimmed to darkness and the curtains rose on the first act. It was a wild-looking guy playing a pair of spoons on his body with orchestral accompaniment, followed by a man who wobbled precariously around the stage while juggling flaming sticks. He failed to impress Larry but made Barry whoop and holler. I guess he was only a kid, in some ways.

Next came Shakin' Stevens, and he greatly entertained Olaf, who had mistakenly believed that Shakey had long since died and saw this as some kind of second coming. He brought the house down by singing This Old House, and even Carla couldn't resist clapping along to Green Door.

So, how could you follow that, except with Mr Know

All, The Human Search Engine – our reason for being there, along with all those gangsters and cops.

'I invite you to ask me anything,' Mr Know All challenged us. The audience got their nonsense questions out of the way first.

'What's best, cheese or sex?' a voice at the back asked.

'Cheese,' he replied.

'Then you're obviously not doing sex right,' the punter replied.

'You've obviously never tasted Wensleydale,' Mr Know All said back, getting plenty of laughs. Who would have believed that this funny and endearing man was about to be whisked away to Russia to recite a secret code that would blight the future of the world forever? I guess he had no idea why he'd been asked to learn the code. I always prefer to think the best of people – just look at me and Inspector Flowers. 'Should I choose Larry or Barry?' I longed to ask him – a no-brainer obviously. A girl in the upper tier asked him to name all the finalists and the ultimate winner of the original series of Pop idol, the UK version of American idol, or so Carla informed me.

An expectant hush fell over the audience, many of whom probably vaguely recalling this particular piece of popular culture.

'Korben, aged 21 from London, eliminated in week one,' he said as a drum roll played under him. 'Rick Waller from Gillingham withdrew in week two, leaving along with Jessica Garlick, aged 20 from Kidwelly, who was eliminated in the same week.'

'Nicely negotiated,' said the sardonic compere, who'd joined him centre stage to assist in this impossible task.

'And in week three, 26-year-old Aaron Bayley from Newcastle was sent home. Week four, 19-year-old Laura Doherty was eliminated. Rosie Ribbons 18, from Altwen, week five, and week six, Hayley Evetts from Birmingham. Zoe, 16, from County Durham in week seven, and in week eight it was Darius Danesh, aged 21, from Glasgow, who got to the end of the road.'

'Feel the love in the room,' said the host.

'And in the final, it was 17-year-old Gareth Gates from Bradford, who finished runner-up to 22-year-old Will Young from Wokingham, who was crowned Winner of Pop Idol 2002,' he announced to gales of applause.

'Now let's really test him,' said Barry Potter.

I knew what I had to do. There was an audible gasp as I rose to my feet, taking off my wig. The Killer In High Heels was in their midst. Flowers and Farage leant over the balcony to watch me do my worst and the police officers started getting ready to place me under arrest.

'Sit down, for God's sake!' said Larry, but it was too late for that.

'Haven't we met before? I never forget a face,' said Mr Know All. 'Yes we have,' he said answering his own question, 'on this very stage, if I'm not mistaken.'

'We have indeed,' I concurred.

'So, what is your question?'

I took a deep breath, aware that I might be shot for asking it.

'Is it possible to live forever?' I simply asked. It seemed to have the effect of sucking all the air from the room.

A look of alarm appeared on Mr Know All's face. 'I'm, er, not sure I should be answering this,' he said. Of course he knew that once he had given the information, it would be deleted from his memory bank.

'Keep your trap shut, and get off stage now!' Farage shouted from the muppet box, but he was almost drowned out by a chorus of boos from the audience below him who demanded that Mr Know All should carry on.

'It's my proud boast that I never fail to answer a question, unless it's football, so I must continue,' he said, addressing his remarks to Farage, who threw up his hands in despair. He inhaled deeply and re-connected with his memory bank, much to the delight of almost everyone there.

'Being able to live forever is about hacking the code of life,' he said. 'The probability of a 25-year-old dying before their 26th Birthday is 0.1%. If we could keep that risk constant throughout life, instead of it rising due to age-related disease, the average person should be able to live for a thousand years.'

'Will you shut the fuck up?' shouted Farage from his box. The compere warned him to be quiet, or otherwise he would be removed from the theatre.

'I will proceed. A group calling itself the Order Of Eternal Life has embarked upon a quest known as The Project, to find a radical solution to the problem of ageing, which should be seen as a curable illness, enabling people to live forever in good health.' You could have heard a molecule of DNA drop. 'Of course, the social implications will be immense, and in order to ensure the continuation of the human race it will be necessary to restrict the benefits to a newly-combined ruling alliance of Trump and Putin, who will rule together in perfect harmony to create a new etenal dynasty forever, to be established as soon as possible.'

'Noooooooo!' cried the audience.

'It's worse than Brexit!' someone else said.

But Barry's reasons were more personal than that, having been betrayed by the Professor. He now got up to ask the million dollar question.

'Mr Know All, can you remember the formula for eternal life?'

'It's this...' said Mr Know All. He proceeded to reel off a series of letters and numbers that meant absolutely nothing to me or the vast majority of the audience, but it clearly meant a great deal to Farage and the Professor.

'Stop him at all costs!' the Professor shouted. At that point some of the audience recognized him as the disgraced scientist doing the Time Warp on the Pointless Halloween Special.

'And to think they used to say the second house at

the Glasgow Empire was tough,' said the compere, but just then a shot rang out and Mr Know All came crashing down on to the stage, apparently lifeless. When I looked up at the muppet box there stood Inspector Flowers, a smoking gun in his hand. He was smiling insanely at me, and I thought I saw him mouth the words 'I love you, Miss Caro,' but before he could elaborate an armed policeman took him out with two rounds from his automatic weapon.

In spite of everything, I could have cried. The audience reacted in horror at having become extras in a shoot out, and panic threatened to engulf us all, had Barry not leapt from his seat and sprinted down the aisle, with me following close behind.

'Please stay calm and remain in your seats to enable the police to enforce the law,' said Barry Potter down the microphone. As he took control as only he could, I leapt onto the stage and started trying to stem the flow of blood from the wound in Mr Know All's stomach before giving him CPR.

'You must allow him to complete the algorithm, Caro,' Barry Potter instructed me, 'because once he's said it it will be wiped from his mind, and the world will be saved.'

'OK, but I'll keep pumping if it's all the same to you,' I said. Mr Know All gradually recovered, and in a shaking voice he resumed his recitation of the formula, coming at last to the final three letters, QED.

'Phew, better out than in,' he said, and fell unconscious

again. Meanwhile the cops had taken control in the hall, arresting both Farage and the Professor, while Flower's lifeless body was already on its way to the morgue. A good man turned bad, or at least that's what I preferred to believe.

And then up stepped Larry. He pushed Barry to one side and held me in his strong arms again, kissing me tenderly on the lips.

'I thought I'd lost you in the shoot-out,' he said.

'And you're OK?'

'He kept his bloody head down in the seats, along with all the other sensible people,' said Olaf. 'Not like our hero Barry Potter, who risked his life for us, and Miss Caro, who saved the nearly fucked memory man.'

'Olaf!' I said, reprimanding him for his use of unfortunate language, but I was more annoyed with him for drawing attention to Barry's heroics at the expense of Larry. If I'd wanted to marry an action hero I would have lined up one of the X Men.

Next I had to endure a significant probing from the real senior officer this time, Inspector Strong, in one of the backstage dressing rooms. He wanted to know all about my adventures and why I'd been forced to flee my home. It didn't take too long to confirm that I was no longer under suspicion of murder, although he reprimanded me for what he described as taking the law into my own hands. That seemed a bit harsh considering I'd just help to save the world despite the efforts of a couple of fake cops.

No sooner had I been declared free to go than Carla announced that she wanted to lock me up again – for my own good of course. She demanded I go into hiding to protect myself from the media, who had become obsessed with my case, not to mention my 38 DDs.

'These people will stop at nothing to get a piece of you. It's for your own safety, Caro,' she said, forgetting to add that it was for her benefit too, so that Capital Talk could have an exclusive on the Killer In High Heels. But surely I owed her that much, having disappeared without warning and left her with a great hole in her schedules. What difference would another couple of days make before Larry and I got together? Carla had insisted I should hide out on my own, and while Larry was less than ecstatic about it, he agreed to wait until all the publicity had died down. I thanked Team Caro for their incredible support, for without Miss Pearl, Olaf and Royston, to say nothing of Barry Potter, I would probably either be six feet under or wrongly imprisoned by the British legal system. I promised to lay on a party for them at the Ritz as soon as I was truly free.

A few days later, in a luxury hide-out at a fabulous five star hotel in the Cotswolds, I sat down to write a heartfelt text to Barry Potter, on the phone that had saved my life, to try and explain my feelings for him. I wrote how he was going to make some woman very happy and said I would always be eternally grateful to him for coming to my rescue in my hour of need. And then I nailed it.

I will never forget you. I will forever be remembered not as the Killer In High Heels, but as the woman who was dumb enough to pass up on the great Barry Potter.

I pressed SEND, and fell asleep.

CHAPTER SIXTEEN

After three days in luxurious captivity I was eventually smuggled out of my hotel and driven by limousine to the studios of Capital Talk, where Carla was waiting. Upon arrival I fought my way through the inevitable scrum and into the sanctuary of the studio, where TV crews and the media waited, all anxious to get a quote from me. Now I knew how it felt to be truly famous – or maybe I should say infamous. Either way I sure as hell didn't much like it.

'You're going on air live at ten,' Carla told me. 'We're expecting our highest ratings ever, with listeners tuning in the world over.'

'No pressure then.'

'I'll be there for you if you need it, otherwise you just

tell the listeners what's been going on in your life, in true Miss Caro style.'

Sounded easy enough, but my heart was pumping worryingly. I was wondering if I had what it takes to present a radio show about something so awe-inspiringly personal as the last few weeks had been. *Just be you*, I kept repeating to myself as the clock ticked towards transmission time, when the whole world would be listening.

At last I heard that familiar deep male voice through my headphones. 'Into the Night – with CAROLINE KENNEDY!'

'Hi there y'all,' I said in my best southern drawl. 'It's good to be back, and in one piece. I bet you've been wondering just what I've been up to, out there, murderin' folks, if you believe everything you've read in the newspapers and on line. Truth is, I've been busy saving the world, according to those geeky scientists. Nothing trivial – a bit like this show I guess. Don't answer that! Now I thought it only fair that you, my long-suffering listeners, should be the first to hear it from me, the horse's mouth, about what in jumping Jehoshaphat has been going on with yours truly.

'I won't be blinding you with all the science stuff – not that I could if I wanted to – except to say that a formula fell into my hands which would make it possible for us all to live forever. Now that might sound fine and dandy, but what would happen to a planet where nobody dies and new ones are born every minute? Meltdown – that's what. President Trump and President Putin colluded in attempting to grab the formula for their own advantage, so they could not only live forever, but rule forever, leaving the rest of us to die, as before.

'I'm glad to report that's no longer possible now, as every copy of the formula has since been destroyed, while Mr Know All no longer has any memory of it, and his recovery is progressing well. Of course Trump has denied having any involvement – well, he would, wouldn't he? – as we wait upon the outcome of the latest FBI investigation into his conduct. Meanwhile, President Putin has been advised to take a long break, going on a hunting holiday – standby for the topless pictures, boys – but he's expected to be back and ruling the roost soon. So, nothing changed really, unlike my personal life.

'Where to start? As I may have once or twice mentioned on the show, Larry, the love of my life, dumped me not long after he proposed marriage, and boy, how I've struggled to get over that, even though it was nearly five years ago. So, with everything else going off, and with nothing else to lose, I finally decided to do something about it. Needless to say, yes Larry and I touched base again. It's always dangerous going back, or so they say, but it felt just as wonderful second time around as I lovingly became re-acquainted with exactly why I loved him so much in the first place. Even more amazingly, Larry felt the same too. Of course, he is nearly twenty years older than me – I've always had a thing about older men, as you listeners well know – yet he was as outstanding as I remembered him, if a little older – well aren't we all? As long as he's all man, who cares about a bit of paunch and a touch of grey?

'But while I was busy sorting out the affairs of my heart, along came a much younger guy, nearly ten years my junior. As if, I hear you cry. But there wasn't anything this young feller couldn't do – fixing algorithmic problems, finding me a temporary job as a nurse, helping me to escape from the law, oh, and fallin' right in love with me in between times. While I don't deny I was flattered, he was still just a boy, and I like real men. And he was decidedly fit for such a young guy with his strong, muscular arms and his beautiful brown skin.

'Now while I'm the first to agree that a relationship between an older woman and a younger guy has much to recommend it – in fact you could argue that its nature's way – I remained besotted with Larry – and it's not all about sex, is it? So as soon as I went into hiding I wasted no time in sending Barry a text to let him down gently. It said, 'I will be forever remembered, not as the Killer In High Heels, but as the woman who was dumb enough to pass up on Barry Potter.

'Trouble is, on waking up in the middle of the night I began to have second thoughts. It wasn't just about Barry being such a hero, or his great body, or knowing how to treat a woman and actually listening to what I said.

It was above all because I could be myself with him. I never had to put on act with Barry, whereas with Larry I was always striving to be somebody I really wasn't – the older woman I wasn't quite yet ready to become. And isn't it everybody's duty 'to thine own self be true,' as Shakespeare once put it? He sure had a way with words. Plus what's more, around the time we were lyin' low in Derbyshire I was beginning to fall under Barry Potter's spell. It didn't damage his cause that he was a fanatasic lover, reaching the parts other guys couldn't reach. But then he said to me, 'I'm not sure if I care about the world any more Miss Caro, if you and I aren't in it together.' How romantic was that?

'So fast forward a few days back to when I was hiding from the press in my hotel, having just rejected him by text. How cruel and insensitive was that? At three o'clock in the morning with nobody there to hear me, I suddenly said out loud, 'I do declare, I love you Barry Potter'. How could I have got it so totally and utterly wrong, confusing Larry with Barry as the love of my life?

'It was only then that I learnt the three best words in the English language aren't 'I love you' but 'message not sent'. That's what I saw when I picked up Barry's phone. I'd been given a second chance. How overjoyed was I?

'As for Larry, maybe we'd just missed our moment in time, and I reckon that deep down, he knew it too. It just wasn't meant to be, and considering all the fuss I've made about him over the years, I can only apologize for that. Larry's not going back to his wife this time though, which is probably for the best – I'm still certain he'll be happier with someone else. And she's hooked up with a much younger man too, while on vacation in the Gambia – it must be catching, ladies.

'So that's all I've got to get off my chest for the moment. The world is saved – at least until the next time. Olaf is still shootin' up and down the freeway – a big shout out to Olaf on the M6! Miss Pearl is working her way towards becoming a headmaster's wife while continuing her broadcasting career as Britain's first ever transgender night-time talk show host, and Barry is waiting for me downstairs – we had to smuggle him in through the side entrance. In truth, the moment I finally worked out that Barry Potter was the one, he came over and joined me at our luxury hotel as fast as a boy wizard on a broomstick, and we cemented our relationship in no uncertain terms. It was one of those places that's licensed to do weddings. So dear listener, I married him.

'And now, time for the weather.'

PART THREE

INTO THE LIGHT

It's not the men in your life that matters,
it's the life in your men.

Mae West

CHAPTER SEVENTEEN

So what should have been a lonely hideout had become a honeymoon in a luxury five-star hotel, courtesy of Capital Talk, Lord bless them – and yes it was still just as heavenly as that little guest house in Derbyshire, if not more so, although I kind of missed the handcuffs. But I've written quite enough about all those goings on, and now that we're married I don't think it would really be seemly for me to go blathering on about our bedtime shenanigans, would it?

All I can say is that everything felt so right in whatever we did together, whether it was making out or walking hand in hand in those magnificent gardens yakking on about this and that. He was surprisingly cool about my frank admission of a newly-found desire for someone of my same sex, namely Wanda in Olaf's truck, although not in that awful creepy 'I'd like to watch' kind of way, but more in a spirit of true understanding of something I might one day need to explore, yet never at the expense of losing us.

Not that we agreed on absolutely everything – that would be boring, wouldn't it? Like when he pulled out that bottle of pills – you know, the ones that give you everlasting life, given to me by Vlad.

'I couldn't bear to be apart from you ever again, Caro. Let's both take one so that we can be together forever.'

I suppose you could say it was like a suicide pact in reverse.

'I'm lovin' the sentiment, Barry,' I replied, 'but I was raised an old-fashioned southern Baptist girl, and for me, the only place to find eternal life is in heaven. It most certainly don't come out of a bottle.'

He looked perplexed. How I loved that particular look, for he still had much to learn, as did we both.

'You'll come round to it in the end. It's just one of the things you need to work on,' I explained.

But he taught me stuff too – like, why do cats always land on their feet if you throw them into the air, or why it's better to be kind than nasty.

He must have trusted me when I tipped those irreplaceable pills down the kitchen sink as if I knew what I was doing. Who wants to live forever, as Freddie once sang? I prefer to live for the moment, however long that might be. Besides, we had another mystery to solve – it now hadn't rained for nearly two months and it didn't seem at all right – not in England's green and pleasant land. But then I heard a gigantic clap of thunder, followed by a torrential downpour of rain, so so we could strike that one off our list.

I had always been more inclined towards solving the mystery of all those female hormones in the sea which could wipe out the male sex at a stroke – now that's pretty darn serious. However, it's an ill wind that don't blow no raccoon out of a peach blossom tree. Just think of all those toilet seats, never left in the upright position ever again.

But I could feel an investigation coming on, just the same.

THE END

BV - #0093 - 220426 - C0 - 203/127/19 - PB - 9781861519160 - Gloss Lamination